As Lonely As
the Damned

A Falcon's Head Mystery

As Lonely As the Damned

John Creasey
as Kyle Hunt

WORLD PUBLISHING

TIMES MIRROR
NEW YORK

Published by The World Publishing Company
Published simultaneously in Canada
by Nelson, Foster & Scott Ltd.

First American edition—1972

WORLD PUBLISHING
TIMES MIRROR

CONTENTS

CHAPTER ONE

Night Call

Dr. Cellini lay sleeping. A shaft of moonlight touching his white hair, gave him the ethereal appearance of a sleeping saint. His wife, Felisa, slept as soundly in the bed beside him. They had long since learned that to sleep well they had to sleep alone, but it was still their custom to start the night and begin the day together; and to have the two close, like this, was the practical as well as the sentimental solution.

The moonlight touched the light covering on Dr. Cellini's small, near-frail figure, but Felisa's bed and the larger outline of her body beneath the thin blanket, was in darkness. The moon, shining on the thick foliage of the trees on the common just outside their window, on shrubs, on grass, on the ornamental pool of this small apartment building, on a yachting pool only half-a-mile away, shone also on London. This place was part of the sprawling city of brick and concrete, of people and palaces, of parks and gardens, of houses built hundreds of years ago and some completed only yesterday. London. On this clear, limpid night one could go to the top of the monstrous Post Office Tower and see for thirty miles in all directions —and only ten miles from that heart of the city lay Dr. Cellini; Emmanuel Cellini, quite oblivious of the fact that, some ten miles to the north of him, a man, a physician, was uttering his name.

'The one man who might be able to help,' this physician was saying, 'is Dr. Cellini.'

Another man, young middle-aged, florid-faced, thick and powerful of torso and shoulder, glared at the physician with bloodshot eyes; deep-set, angry and red-rimmed.

'Then send for this Cellini,' he growled; his expression that of one issuing an order.

'I will, in the morning,' the doctor promised.

'What the hell are we going to gain by waiting until the morning? She's ill *now*.'

'My dear Robert,' the physician said, patiently. 'Nothing Dr. Cellini, or anyone else, can do can make any difference for a few hours. Your wife is under sedation and won't come round until the morning. If you wish me to consult him, I will, but shouldn't you know something about him, first?'

'I know all I want to know about him,' Gregory declared. 'He's that quack psychiatrist who—'

'Robert,' interrupted the physician, 'Dr. Cellini is as fully qualified as I, and he is certainly not a quack.'

Gregory stirred impatiently.

'You're all quacks,' he sneered.

'Do you really think it is going to do Melinda any good if you antagonise everyone who would like to help you?' The physician, a tall, middle-aged aquiline-featured man who was sitting upright in an easy chair in a large, well-appointed drawing-room, had a square chin and eyes which could sharpen as his voice was sharpening now. 'There are times when I wonder whether you really want her to get better.'

His words fell into a silence broken only by Robert Gregory's heavy breathing. The broad nostrils of the rather short nose widened. The deep-set eyes seemed to glow like smouldering embers. He took two steps forward, so that he was towering over the physician, his hands, pale and well-shaped, clenched by his side.

'What the hell do you mean by that?'

'I mean exactly what I say.'

'I spend a fortune on doctors and nursing homes trying to

get my wife back to health!'

'You have a dozen fortunes,' retorted the physician, acidly. 'So what you spend on Melinda is neither sacrifice nor effort.'

'My God, you've got a nerve!' cried Gregory, and he looked as if he might swing his arms and drag the other to his feet. The physician showed no sign of fear; indeed, he settled back in his chair, while Gregory glowered and maintained his menacing pose. He was breathing heavily, his lips parted enough to show his small, very white, even teeth. He drew a deep breath. 'You know damned well that I would spend every penny I've got to make her well.'

Very coldly, the physician said, 'I doubt it.'

There was a pause, in which tension seemed to grow. The silence was broken only by Gregory's breathing. Then he rose on his toes, and the physician settled further back in his chair. Suddenly, like a savage animal, Gregory sprang, hands stretched out, lips wide apart, teeth clenched. The physician swung his legs to one side, and Gregory crashed into the chair arm. There was a strange, soughing of air being forced out of stomach and lungs, as he doubled up, toppling forward until his head was almost in the physician's lap. The physician simply lowered his legs. Gregory, breath coming in short, squeaky gasps, lolled sideways and fell to the floor. His face was ashen grey with the pain. He drew his knees up to his chin and clutched his legs with his arms, then lay inert, his whole body quivering.

The physician leaned down and felt his pulse; it was very fast. He leaned over and loosened Gregory's waistband, then pulled down the elastic at the top of his pants, loosened his collar and tie and unfastened his shirt cuffs. He did all of this very quickly and detachedly, and when it was done, straightened up and looked down at the quivering body. After a few moments, he went out of the room, entering a spacious hall the walls of which were adorned for the most part, with contemporary paintings. Here and there could be

seen a Picasso, a Matisse, a Van Gogh. Every piece of furniture was either antique or by a contemporary master, every
bronze a work worthy of exhibiting in any museum. There
was only one trouble in this hall; it had the coldness, the
aloofness, of a museum. 'Do not touch the Exhibits' seemed
to be written in invisible letters on every wall.

The physician stood for moment looking round, and then
went along a passage at the side of a staircase which had
half-landings, then a narrower staircase in each direction.
Along this passage was a doorway which stood ajar, and the
physician tapped. Immediately there was a bustle of movement, and an elderly man appeared in the doorway.

'Dr. Selwin!'

'Don't worry,' the physician said.

'But how *is* Mrs. Gregory, sir?'

'She is sleeping, with a sedative,' answered Dr. Selwin,
'and she won't wake until the morning.' He entered a room
where a middle-aged, apple-cheeked woman was standing at
a square table, hands clasped in front of her, obviously very
troubled. Selwin nodded reassurance, and the anxiety in her
face eased. 'But I'm afraid Mr. Gregory isn't well.'

The man said, 'Oh, dear.'

The woman hesitated, and then asked, 'Is he *very* ill,
doctor?'

'I don't think so. Will you get his bed ready and heat some
milk? You come with me, Popple.'

The pair took the physician's orders without hesitation,
and as he and Popple turned left, towards the hall and the
room where Gregory was, Popple's wife turned in the opposite direction, towards the kitchen. The physician went into
the room, and saw Gregory kneeling in front of the chair
where he, the physician, had been sitting. It was a large,
square room, in pale greens and blues, with two walls filled
to the ceiling with books which had their wrappers on, adding to the colour, making it more a woman's room than a

man's. Facing the door, and set square, was a large pedestal desk of pale oak. Matching tables and chairs stood close to it. This end of the room, near the door, had low tables, low, luxurious chairs in pale leather, and on the shelves some bronzes which matched the beauty of those in the hall.

Gregory was still gasping.

Popple hesitated for a moment and then turned to Selwin. There was a question in his eyes but none on his lips. Gregory was obviously unaware that they were present, and was making a great effort to get to his feet. The two men crossed over to him.

'You help on that side, Ben.'

'Very good, sir,'

'Take it easy,' Selwin said to Gregory. 'We'll help you.'

The man on his knees glanced round, hardly moving his head. His mouth was wide open, his eyes narrowed, his tongue showed as he breathed; or more truly, panted. There was no expression on his face except of exhaustion. The others took him by each arm, just beneath the armpit, and eased him to his feet. He was a dead weight, and as they went towards the door, his feet dragged and he made no effort to help himself. But by the time they reached the stairs, he was taking a little weight on his legs. They took him along a passage on the other side of the staircase from the one where the Popples had their room. Built into the side of the staircase was a lift large enough for two.

'I'll go up the stairs, sir,' Popple said.

Selwin nodded, and helped Gregory into the lift, squeezed in and pressed the button. The lattice-work iron gates closed gently and they crawled up. When they reached the next floor, Gregory was standing without support. The lift stopped and Popple appeared at the gate.

He moved to help Gregory, who muttered, 'I'm all right,' in a sullen voice, and turned towards the left. He was only a few steps away when he stumbled and lurched forward.

Selwin took his arm and led him into a bedroom on the right. It was a long, narrow room, looking out over a garden floodlit in several delicate colours. Mrs. Popple was at the window, drawing the curtains. The big, double bed was turned down, and by its side was a table with a glass of steaming hot milk and some crackers.

Gregory stared at the woman.

'Get out,' he ordered in a hoarse voice.

The woman's lips tightened, and she strode out, head held high. Popple's eyes sparked but he said nothing.

'Don't want any help,' Gregory muttered. 'From anyone.' Now his gaze swivelled from Popple to Selwin and back. Popple inclined his head, muttered something that sounded like, 'Very good, sir,' and followed his wife. He left the door ajar. Gregory dropped to the side of the bed and bent down to unfasten his shoes. He managed to get one unlaced, then began to topple forward. Selwin supported him. Very gently he said, 'Let me help, Bob.'

'I don't want—' Gregory began, and then gulped. 'Oh, hell!' he muttered. 'I hate you. I hate Melinda. I hate the Popples. I hate the whole bloody world and everyone in it. To hell with you all.' He kicked at Selwin, who moved back quickly, and made a tremendous effort to stand up. *'Get out!'* he rasped. 'And don't come back. I'm through with you. *Through.*' He contrived to look almost dignified but at the same time more than a little ridiculous as he raised a quivering arm towards the door.

'Very well,' Selwin said, quietly. He looked at the other levelly for a few seconds and then turned slowly away. The door was at the other end of the room. As he walked towards it, tall, lean, and with a kind of elegance, Gregory watched him, his lips beginning to quiver. He stretched out a hand, fingers crooked, in silent appeal. Selwin reached the door and opened it wider, stepped through and turned towards the stairs.

Gregory gave a peculiar little croaking sound, but did not move until Selwin disappeared. Then he staggered towards the door, calling out, 'Jacob! Jacob!'

Selwin did not call back.

Gregory reached the door, held on to it to keep his balance, and called in a louder and clearer voice, 'Jacob!'

Jacob Selwin was at the stairs, already a step down, but able to see Gregory who took a few more stumbling steps towards him, calling his name. For a moment he stood there, as if making up his mind whether to respond or not. The expression on Gregory's face was piteous.

'Ja-Jacob! I'm—sorry. I didn't—mean—' he broke off, choking.

Very slowly Selwin turned back, and the relief on Gregory's face was pitiful to see. He stepped sideways to the wall and leaned against it, waiting for Selwin, who took his arm and led him back to the bedroom.

'I—I didn't mean it,' Gregory muttered. 'Jacob, don't —don't ever leave me. I—I'm impossible I know but— but—I need help. You know I do. You're the only man I can talk to, the only man I can confide in. Don't—don't walk out on me.'

He looked up into Selwin's lean, sharp-featured face, his own face, so broad in contrast, now pale and frightened. They stood still for several seconds, before Selwin said, 'I can't help you any more, Bob.'

'Oh, God! Don't say that!' Gregory stretched out his arms imploringly.

'It's the simple truth. I can't help you any more.' stated Selwin in a calm, positive voice. 'I've done everything I can both as friend and physician, but I'm at the end of my skill with you. You need—'

'*I won't see a psychiatrist!*' cried Gregory with a flare of defiance. 'How many more times do I have to tell you I'm not mad?'

'You need help from someone with much wider experience than I have,' replied Selwin. 'If you won't listen to me I shall have to stop treating you altogether. You're too big a responsibility.'

Gregory gulped.

'You—you *do* think I'm mad, don't you?'

'No,' denied Selwin. 'I do think you are suffering from some kind of tension I don't quite understand, and that if you go on as you are you'll have a nervous breakdown. If you let that happen, God knows whether you'll ever recover.'

Gregory muttered, 'They're a lot of damned quacks!'

'Some of them are, perhaps, but the man I want you to see isn't. He's an elderly practitioner with most extensive experience in dealing with all kinds of people, and he is perhaps the wisest man I know. I think you'll learn to trust him. I hate to say it, but I think this man is your only hope.'

Gregory looked away, and muttered, 'I'll think about it. Let me have a couple of sleeping pills, and I'll sleep on it.' A cunning glint crept into his eyes as he turned to look at Selwin.

Slowly, the physician shook his head.

'No more pills, no more treatment from me unless I can consult Dr. Cellini,' he said flatly. 'And no more waiting or procrastination, either. I shall walk out and not come back unless you will see Cellini tonight.'

'Tonight!' screeched Gregory. 'But it's in the middle of the night! No psychiatrist would come at this time.'

'Dr. Cellini will, if I ask him to,' said Selwin. 'I wouldn't have disturbed him for Melinda, but I want him to see you after one of these attacks of hysteria. It's now or never, Robert.'

The two men faced each other in challenge; then suddenly Gregory raised his arms on a level with his shoulders and then let them flop in a helpless gesture of resignation.

*   *   *

Dr. Cellini stirred at the sound of the telephone. Starting up, he stretched out his arm quickly, and lifted the receiver. He did not answer at once but eased himself higher on his pillow as he glanced at his sleeping wife. The moonlight had shifted so that now it only fell on the top of his silvery hair.

'This is Dr. Cellini,' he stated. 'Who!' he asked, and listened for a few moments, before saying, 'Yes, I remember you telling me about him. If in your considered opinion this is the appropriate time, I will most certainly come . . . What address? . . . Hethersett, Hethersett Drive, Hampstead? . . . No, I don't know it, but . . . Yes indeed, I know the pond, if you will meet me there it will be most helpful . . . In thirty minutes, say? . . . Very well, Dr. Selwin . . . I only hope that I can help.'

CHAPTER TWO

The Pond

Dr. Jacob Selwin stood by the side of his sleek, grey Jensen, one of the luxuries he allowed himself, and watched the ripples in the pond and the shimmering reflection of a waning moon obscured at odd moments by fleecy clouds. The wind was pleasant, and the scent of new mown grass from a near-by house where the lawns must have been cut that evening, was almost heady. Now and again a car swept up the hill from Swiss Cottage or from the roads to the right, the left or behind him, headlights swaying. He was familiar with Manny Cellini's old car, which would come slowly, almost sedately, up the hill. He had been here for ten minutes so Manny was ten minutes late, rare for him.

A car came from behind Selwin and swung to a standstill. He saw the word 'Police' on a sign on the roof. A man got out and came towards him.

'Good evening, sir.'

'Good evening,' Selwin said, puzzled.

'Is everything all right, sir?'

'Perfectly,' Selwin said. 'I am waiting for a friend.'

The officer's eyebrows shot up.

'At two o'clock in the morning?'

Selwin laughed.

'Yes. It must seem a little odd, I suppose. I am a doctor, waiting to see a specialist, and I want a word with him before we meet our patient. And he's late—' He broke off, glancing down the hill as a car appeared; and when it passed beneath a street lamp he recognised the comparatively square top and the heavy brasswork of a vintage Morris; the street lamplight also shimmered on the high polish of the car. 'Here he is,' Selwin added, and chuckled. 'I'm quite serious. I assure you that I *am* about to have a quick preliminary consultation with Dr. Cellini.'

'Dr. *Who*, sir?'

'Cellini—Emmanuel Cellini.'

'Oh, Manny!' the policeman said, and he laughed in turn. 'Sorry to have troubled you, sir. Good night.'

He went off, on Selwin's 'good night' and to the note of the engine of Manny Cellini's car. Selwin felt very slightly rueful that Cellini, who lived on the other side of London, should be immediately recognised while he, who lived only on the other side of the Heath, should have gone unrecognised. But that didn't matter. Here was Manny, pulling up just behind him. Selwin stepped to the side of the car as the police car drove off, and Cellini opened his door, saying in a gentle voice, 'Good evening, Jacob.'

'Hallo, Manny. Very good of you to come out so late.'

'Not at all. Did I perceive the minions of the law?'

'They were suspicious of me,' Selwin told him. 'Probably thought I was contemplating suicide. May I sit with you for a few moments before we go on to the house?'

'By all means,' agreed Cellini obligingly.

He was a small man compared with Selwin, and the light from the street lamps shone on his silvery moustache and hair and his pale face, which looked faintly yellow. He was thin on top, but not bald. His features were fine and his expression was gentle. There was a slightly formal note in his voice and in his diction, for he was not even first generation English but had come here from Italy in his early teens.

Selwin appeared to have some difficulty in starting, so Cellini asked, 'How long has this man you wish me to see been your patient?'

'Twenty years,' answered Selwin.

Cellini glanced at him as if in surprise.

'That is a very long time. What has caused the acute change?'

'There hasn't been one,' the other answered, and before Cellini could comment he went on with a hint of laughter, 'After twenty years, I bring you out in the middle of the night!' He paused, before going on thoughtfully, 'Perhaps there has been an acute change, after all.'

'Ah,' murmured Dr. Cellini.

'He agreed to see you,' went on Selwin.

'And he has been bitterly opposed to seeing a psychiatrist?'

'Yes.'

'Does he fear that he will be adjudged insane?' inquired Cellini mildly.

'That is exactly what he fears.'

'How long have you thought he needed my help?' asked Cellini.

'For nearly a year,' Selwin answered.

Cellini did not respond immediately and there was a hint of reproof in his silence and in his quiet response, 'You have known he needed help but could not persuade him to seek it for nearly a *year*?'

Selwin answered, 'That is so,' and sat in silence.

It was Cellini who spoke next.

'Is he very wealthy?'

'Very. Certainly a multi-millionaire.' Selwin paused as if to allow time for that to register, but went on before Cellini could respond, 'What made you think he is wealthy?'

Cellini smiled at him, a glint in his eyes.

'In the first place, he is a patient of yours.'

'Oh, that's hard,' protested Selwin.

'But surely true,' Cellini murmured, 'although I do know of your work at the Welfare Centres, Jacob. I am only teasing. However—a patient of yours whom you permit to procrastinate for a year, *must* be wealthy!'

'Or I would have told him to find another doctor, you mean?'

'That is exactly what I mean,' agreed Cellini.

'Less than fair,' protested Selwin. 'I've known him for a long time, even before I was his doctor I was his—' there was only the slightest of hesitation before he went on, 'friend.'

'*His* friend?'

'A friend of his family. And—' again there was a fractional pause before Selwin went on, 'and his wife's family.'

'I see. A wealthy man and a wealthy wife. Wealthy in her own right I imagine.'

'Yes,' agreed Selwin, giving a ghost of a laugh. 'Manny, *I'm* not your patient. Yet, at all events!' He paused again. 'He is Robert Gregory, of Gregory and Wolf, commercial bankers. He married Melinda, a daughter of the Wolf partner in the business. The Wolfs and the Gregorys merged their businesses fifteen years ago, about the time of the marriage. Gregory is now forty-nine. Sometimes he looks it, but when he is well and happy he could pass for forty or even under.'

'I see,' remarked Cellini. 'And does his unhappiness arise through his wife?'

'Yes.'

'How old is Melinda?' inquired Cellini.

'Thirty-five,' answered Selwin. 'Although she won't often admit it. She's a beauty who can sometimes be taken for thirty.'

'Ah. She is reticent about her age—and, I imagine, unfaithful.'

Selwin said, 'You really *are* uncanny!'

'Oh, come,' protested Cellini. 'A man is married to a wealthy and beautiful woman some fifteen years younger than he, and his unhappiness springs from her. So: she gives him cause. So: she is probably unfaithful.' After a long pause he asked quite sharply, 'Often?'

'Often what?'

'Is she often unfaithful?'

'Why don't you guess that too?' invited Selwin.

'If I had to guess, I would say quite often,' said Cellini.

'Tell me why you think so,' said Selwin curiously.

Cellini turned his head and seemed to imply, 'Do you really have to be told?' He did not answer for some time, and in the pause two cars passed in the same direction, going very fast, and then a motor-cyclist went in the other direction, slowly, while—unexpectedly—two men walked by briskly, staring at the couple in the car. Only when their footsteps had faded did Cellini answer.

'You have known he was in distress and in need of psychiatric help for nearly a year. He must have been building up to the time when his need became apparent for some months. He is very wealthy and judging from what you tell me, in love with his wife, and he has been repressing his emotions for a long time.' Cellini paused, pursing his lips. 'If it were a long standing *affaire*, he would probably have adjusted or rebelled. So, I imagine that there might be a sequence of *affaires* to which he simply cannot adjust.' Cellini stopped, and glanced sideways, as if for confirmation.

Slowly, Selwin nodded.

'A great many *affaires*,' he stated simply. 'But—' His voice trailed off.

'But you find the circumstances extenuating?' asked Cellini, gently.

'In a way I do,' admitted Selwin. 'But I don't set too

much store on extenuating circumstances in marital infidelity. One day the western world is going to develop a society which admits and accepts that the human being is not naturally or instinctively monogamous. Some may be, but the desire not to be is very strong in most even if the desire is repressed. And if it's repressed too much or over too long a period and there is little sex life between man and wife, you get a Robert Gregory.'

'Oh, dear,' said Cellini, as if shocked. 'We appear to have a promiscuous woman and a monogamous man bound together in uneasy wedlock.' He twirled the ends of his moustache. 'What has brought on the present crisis? Yet another man in Melinda Gregory's life?'

'Yes,' answered Selwin, simply.

'And Gregory discovered it tonight?'

'Yes. Apparently there was a shocking scene,' said Selwin. 'The servants, a couple named Popple, overheard all and saw part of it . . . I'm not unused to rows and scenes between the Gregorys, and others for that matter, but if Mrs. Popple is right—and she was nearly hysterical when she called me—this was the scene of scenes.'

*　　*　　*

Maxine Popple knew the Gregorys well, and she had worked for them since their marriage. She had often been shocked and even horrified by what went on, but that evening had been bad beyond all conception. She could still close her eyes and press her forefingers against her ears and still both see and hear the man and the woman in such fiery, savage, near-animal fury, that she had been afraid that murder would be done.

It had begun so quietly; so innocently.

It was one of the few evenings when both the Gregorys were at home. They had had dinner and were having coffee in the library, the 'master's' room—and Popple, who was emptying some ashtrays and putting away empty cocktail glasses and bottles, heard Melinda say, 'I won't be coming to Athens, Robert.'

There was tautness in her voice; obviously she anticipated trouble. Gregory, until that moment relaxed in a chair opposite his wife, coffee in hand, started so much that the coffee spilt in his saucer.

'Don't be absurd. Of course you're coming.'

'It won't be possible,' Melinda asserted.

Popple could see her when he turned from drawing the curtains. She was a striking beauty; dark-haired, with an olive-coloured complexion, brilliant hazel brown eyes, beautifully shaped lips. She had rather high cheekbones, a broad forehead, a square chin with a slight cleft.

Popple heard, 'It won't be possible,' and then caught the whistling sound of Gregory drawing in his breath. He could see his employer's profile, the broad nose, the rather thick, curled lips. He had often seen the lines at the other's mouth when his jaw went tight with rage, as it did now; and the pallor, broken by a spot of red, told its own story. Stiffly, Popple walked past but he did not think either of the others realised he was there.

'You'll bloody well come,' Gregory rasped.

'I can't and I won't,' said Melinda.

'You'll come if I have to drag you by the hair.'

'Quite the brave man,' Melinda sneered. 'You might be able to drag some of your staff or your friends by the hair, but—'

'Once and for all,' Gregory said, 'you are coming on the *Baretta* to Athens. You are going to be the hostess on board my yacht for once. You are going to behave as if you were my wife, instead of some little slut who's been picked off the streets.'

Popple had gone, now. No one but Melinda and Gregory was there, and only Gregory could see the way Melinda's lips began to twitch at the corners, how her eyes began to glare instead of shine.

'I won't talk to you in this mood,' she said thinly.

He strode across to her chair and glared down, much as he was to do, a few hours afterwards, with Jacob Selwin. His right fist was raised and clenched.

'You're coming to Athens, you—'

She began to gasp for breath, and shouted, 'Keep away from me!'

He stood so that she could not move, spread the fingers of his right hand so that they were like stubby claws, and buried them in her hair. He gripped, she gasped, he thrust her head back so that her flawless neck was stretched to its utmost. Fear flared in her eyes, her lips were parted, showing her curled tongue.

'You're coming to Athens!' he screeched. 'Just for once you can pass up your new boy-friend. *I'll* sleep with you for a change!'

She kicked him savagely on the shin, and he gasped and let her go. But as she darted towards the door he grabbed her arm and yanked her back, still glaring. They stood like that, Gregory panting, Melinda's breathing coming in short, harsh gasps.

*   *   *

Popple dared to peer through the gap at the doorway.

He heard Gregory rasp, 'Who is it, this time? Come on, tell me, who is it?' He saw Melinda stagger away, then turn and run towards the door. He opened it wide so that she could run through, away from her husband, who chased after her.

As she started up the stairs Melinda began to shout. When she reached her bed she flung herself on it and screamed and screeched and kicked her legs so furiously that when Gregory reached the doorway even he was appalled.

Coming upstairs, step at a time, fearfully, was Mrs. Popple.

In the hall, Popple was telephoning Dr. Selwin's house, and when told that Selwin was out begged his wife to find him and send him to Hethersett.

'I'm afraid Mrs. Gregory will die,' he said hoarsely. 'I'm really afraid she'll die.'

CHAPTER THREE

Sleeping Beauty

Dr. Cellini listened to Selwin's recital of events with absorbing interest, and when it was finished, nodded slightly, smoothing his moustache with the thumb and forefinger of his left hand. Selwin moistened his lips, then took out cigarettes, but suddenly paused and dropped the case back into his pocket. Cellini, still in a kind of reverie, did not appear to notice.

'So she is thoroughly promiscuous?' he remarked at last.

'She appears to be,' answered Selwin.

'Do you—ah—know her well, too?'

'They have been married for fifteen years, and I've attended her throughout the whole period.'

'Did you know her before?'

'Not as a doctor.'

'Just as a family friend?'

'No,' answered Selwin, but doubt seemed to hover in the word.

'An acquaintance, perhaps?' Cellini now turned his whole body to look at Selwin, whose face was half-bright, half-shadowed in the uneven glow thrown by a street lamp. His eyes glistened; the set of his mouth was thin and taut.

'We moved in the same social circle, the same group, but we were never close friends.'

'Was she—ah—liberal with her favours then?'

'I didn't think so, at the time.'

'Exactly what time?' asked Cellini.

'Sixteen or seventeen years ago,' answered Selwin. 'She was very beautiful.' Cellini made an encouraging gesture and he went on, 'Beautiful, vivacious, very happy provided she was the centre of attraction which she usually was.' He paused, and gave a short laugh. 'I'm being less than just to her, Manny. For a very rich young woman she was as unspoiled as she could be. Everyone did crowd round her, she was the centre of the younger set in the group. I was in the older set. She was—fluttery. She wouldn't take any man seriously, wouldn't go steady, as the saying is. It was a complete surprise to everyone when she married Bob Gregory.'

'A love match?' murmured Cellini.

'There could hardly have been any other reason. They met as a result of the merger, it wasn't a marriage of convenience.'

'Were the families associated in any way apart from business?'

'No. I don't think I told you that Melinda's father was an American. He made his money out of oil, then went into banking. Although half-American, Melinda's lived in England most of her life. Bob has always been in banking—the Gregorys began at the same time as the Rothschilds!' He laughed again. 'He and Melinda moved in the same circles, though. Millionaire circles.'

'Was there any opposition to the marriage?' asked Cellini.

'Not as far as I know.'

'Was it happy at first?'

'As far as I know.' Selwin's answers seemed to form a refrain. 'They went off on a world trip which lasted for over a year, and I was out of England for the better part of six months after they came back. Her parents were killed in an aircrash only a few days after I saw them again.'

His voice faded, and Cellini's gentle, 'How very sad,'

seemed almost loud. 'Was Melinda acutely distressed?'

'Yes, acutely. I was called in and put her under sedation for three days,' Selwin told him. 'Bob was badly upset and very edgy about Melinda. That was the first time I was really aware there was some kind of trouble. When she began to come round there were little quarrels—sharp exchanges, both of them being quick to anger. I can remember Bob saying to me, "God knows what she'll be like after this", and when I asked what he meant, he said that she was always on edge, very excited and in high spirits one moment but liable to change her mood at the drop of a hat. Apparently she'd had a miscarriage in Japan.'

'Ah,' said Cellini. 'A miscarriage and the loss of her parents in the space of a few months. Did you talk to her about this?'

'I consulted Sir Henry Williamson,' Selwin answered. 'He prescribed some hard work!'

'How like Williamson,' murmured Cellini, nodding. 'But she was never given the treatment, presumably.'

Selwin laughed.

'I don't know what would have happened had Bob tried it. She did recover, or she appeared to, but it was about a year later when he told me that she was having an *affaire*. He was nearly out of his mind, and—' Selwin gave a rueful, almost bitter smile, 'I think he's been nearly out of his mind ever since.'

'Yet he stayed with her, in this age of divorce,' Cellini remarked.

'Manny,' said Selwin, earnestly. 'He is still as much in love with her as he was when they married. And he's still as proud of possessing her, owning her as it were, as he was then, too. I don't really know what's gone on in his mind, but I do know that at times it's been anguish. Only in the past year has it seemed to me that he was getting very much worse, living more and more on his nerves. And if that sounds corny—'

'It doesn't sound corny at all,' Cellini interrupted. 'But improbable, perhaps, that a man could live for so long in such circumstances.'

'I know at least two couples who live in almost the same circumstances—a happily married set-up to all outward appearances, although each will have lovers almost *ad infinitum*,' said Selwin. 'And I'm quite sure none of them has emotional or psychological problems.'

Cellini looked at him very straightly.

'If they haven't, they have adjusted to the new society,' he remarked, 'and they are very lucky. However, if one has not adjusted then this changes the circumstances. Does Robert Gregory take drugs?' The question came very sharply.

'No. I've given him digitalin for his heart occasionally, and he always carries some digitalin tablets, but he's not a drug addict.'

'Can you be absolutely certain?'

'I've taken every kind of test—blood, urine, hair, skin. The only drugs he ever takes are those which I prescribe for him, and I'm very careful with those, especially the digitalin. In some ways,' added Selwin, taking out his cigarettes and lighting one without a second thought for Cellini's fastidiousness, 'Bob Gregory is a remarkable man. I've never known anyone with stronger willpower. He will hang on like grim death when most other men would simply give up. He was once caught in a squeeze between two larger bankers and his fellow directors wanted to sell out, but Bob bought them out and held on. He won. Today he is undisputedly in control of one of the strongest commercial banks, a consultant to the Treasury and the Bank of England. As a batsman he has played right through an innings more times than anyone I can remember.'

'So he has never been a man to give up easily,' Cellini

remarked. 'Perhaps we should go and see him, now. Had you given him any sedative before you left?'

'I didn't think you'd want him tranquillised.'

'No indeed,' approved Cellini. 'If you will drive ahead of me, Jacob, not too fast at the corners, please.'

The two cars were driven sedately from the pond to Hethersett. The night was calm and dark yet the shapes of the trees showed clearly. Street lamps, though bright, were few and far between, and Gregory's house appeared as a blaze of light, visible at first through the branches of trees and shrubs. It was very wide, with huge windows from which the lights blazed; the porch was floodlit, windows and the sides and the first floor were ablaze, too. Light made the leaves of the nearer trees pale and translucent, and was gradually swallowed up in the shadows of the heavier branches. The wheels of the two cars crunched on an immaculate gravel drive. Selwin pulled up beyond the porch, Cellini in front of it. As the two men met on the porch itself, Cellini asked wonderingly, 'Is it always lit up like a fairground?'

'It wasn't when I left,' Selwin said, sharp alarm in his voice. 'I hope to God nothing's gone wrong.'

He stepped to the door. It opened and Popple stood there with a shotgun in his left hand. Light shone behind him and, from the porch, on to his face, showing his round eyes bright with fear, his ashen pallor.

'What the devil's the matter?' Selwin demanded, striding in.

'There—there are men in the grounds,' Popple gasped. 'Two men, at least, they—they tried to climb up to Madam's room. I put on all the lights to scare them away, but they're watching, I'm sure they're watching.'

'Did Mr. Gregory tell you—'

'Mr. Gregory went out, sir,' interrupted Popple. 'He—he was in a very bad temper, he said he didn't want to see any more doctors, he said he wouldn't come back. Dr. Selwin, I really don't think my wife and I can stay here alone. We've done everything we can, our nerves are torn to pieces. Can't you make some arrangements for Mrs. Gregory to go away so that we are free to leave?'

*   *   *

To Emmanuel Cellini, the scene was most bizarre.

The story he had heard from Selwin, the bright lights, the terror on the old man's face, the story of the men in the grounds and now the disappearance of the man he had come to see, all added to the weirdness. And this beautifully furnished hall with its over-bright lights had a special kind of eeriness. Selwin looked absolutely flabbergasted; Cellini had never before seen him out of countenance.

'But he *can't* have gone.'

'I assure you he has, sir,' Popple insisted in an unsteady voice.

'He knew—' began Selwin, and then gulped. 'Did he take his car?'

'Yes, sir. I saw him drive off.'

'But—' began Selwin, and then stopped and made a palpable effort to pull himself together. 'How is Mrs. Gregory?'

'My wife is sitting with her, sir, we didn't feel that she should be left alone. Will you go and see her, please?'

'I would very much like to see her,' Cellini interposed.

Selwin led the way upstairs, and as Cellini followed he heard the old man shooting the bolts at the front door. This whole household was immersed in fear. Selwin knew his way about well, and was obviously very familiar with passages and doorways. Along a wide passage a door stood open with light streaming out on to a wall and a Constable landscape, recognisable at a glance. As Selwin turned into the doorway, a woman sprang up from a rocking chair near a double four-poster bed draped with pale yellow silk.

On the bed lay another woman, a beautiful one, sleeping.

From the chair came the first woman, elderly and scared-looking, breathing very hard.

'Doctor, I can't stand this any longer. I really can't. I love Miss Melinda, I would do anything for her, but this awful tension night after night, it's dreadful. It really is. I simply can't stand it another night!'

She was quivering, obviously as fear-stricken as her husband.

'Now don't get excited, Maxine, everything will be all right,' Selwin soothed.

'That's what you always say, but instead of getting better it gets worse. I've never had a night like tonight and I simply can't stand it.' Her voice quivered, her whole body was ashake, and yet she kept her voice low and as she finished glanced over her shoulder at the sleeping beauty.

Melinda Gregory really was beautiful.

She had dark hair, spread about her head on a gold-coloured pillow, like a halo. It looked as if it had been set, or at least freshly brushed and combed, after she had gone to bed. She lay on her back, one arm over the bedspread, the other underneath the gold-coloured sheet. Her lips were closed; well-shaped, soft, seductive-looking lips; and her complexion was so perfect it was like peach bloom. Her eyelashes, dark as her hair, swept down exaggeratedly, but they did not seem false.

Cellini saw all of these things in a glance, and faced Maxine Popple again as Selwin replied sharply, 'Maxine, you are forgetting yourself.'

'On the contrary for the first time I am *thinking* of myself,' Maxine Popple retorted. There was something about the set of her lips which told of absolute determination, just as there was something in the quivering tension of her lined face and body which told of a compulsive fear. Cellini glanced at Selwin and saw his lips tighten and his eyes glint; in the past few minutes he had become an angry man, and it would not take much more to make him lose his temper.

'Dr. Selwin,' Cellini said, mildly, 'perhaps Mrs. Popple doesn't realise that you have consulted me—I am Dr. Cellini, Mrs. Popple—because you are fully aware that things can't go on as they are.' He smiled, benignly, first at Selwin and then at the woman, who was immediately taken aback. 'And we will both need and value your advice,' he went on to Mrs. Popple. 'I wonder if, while we are examining Mrs. Gregory, you could make me a cup of tea. I am not as young as I used to be, and the early hours of the morning don't find me at my best.'

He looked like an elderly cherub as he spoke, and slowly her tension eased and the lines in her face seemed to soften. She gulped once or twice, and then nodded, glanced at Melinda, and began to bustle out.

'I'm very glad you've come to help,' she said, and added from the doorway, 'Shall I bring the tea in when it's ready, or will you ring?'

'Bring it as soon as it's ready, please,' requested Cellini.

She went out, and Selwin raised both hands in the air and gave a smile that was half-wondering and half-exasperated. As Mrs. Popple's footsteps faded, he asked in an almost cynical way, 'Do you mesmerise them or is it simply your natural charm, Manny? It's a long time since I've seen her so amenable.'

'She was troubled and we soothed her,' Cellini said. 'Jacob, how worried are you about Robert Gregory? Is there any likelihood that he will do something silly?'

'Such as?'

'Commit suicide,' suggested Cellini.

'I wouldn't give it a thought,' Selwin assured him. 'I've known him storm out of the house in the past, but he always comes back before long. He may well be at his club. You can be sure he will be at his office at a quarter to ten in the morning. But he'll probably refuse to see you after this, and I'm even more sure he needs you.'

'Does his wife?' asked Cellini.

Both men turned to look at Melinda, who had not stirred and who seemed to be sleeping naturally. Cellini became aware of Selwin looking at him, and glanced away. As he did so the window came into his line of vision, and with a wild start, he saw a man's head and shoulders there. The man, apparently oblivious of him and of Selwin, was staring at the sleeping woman.

CHAPTER FOUR

The Man at the Window

Selwin, seeing the change in Cellini's expression and the way he stared, turned his head, and then cried out, 'Good God!' He spun round towards the window. Cellini checked him in a low-pitched voice.

'Jacob. Please!'

'But—that man!'

'Go out and try to detain him,' Cellini urged. 'You won't have a chance if you try to open the window.'

Selwin turned towards the door, but the man at the window did not appear to notice, certainly did not shift his gaze as Selwin went out. Cellini moved closer to the bed, averting his eyes yet memorising the face. It was the rounded face of a young man who had dark hair and a pronounced widow's peak. He appeared to be standing on a ladder centred on the lower window ledge, and there was not even a hint of excitement in him. He just watched Melinda, calmly.

Cellini ignored him, and felt Melinda's pulse. She was pleasantly warm, her skin was without blemish, and her arm was seductively rounded. Her pulse was rather slow, as was to be expected, but otherwise normal. He let her arm fall lightly, then touched her right eyelid, raising it. The light was such that it showed the pale brown, or hazel colour of her eyes, but although the colouring was lovely, the eye seemed 'dead' and the pupil was a pin-point. He lowered the lid and turned towards the window.

The man had gone.

Cellini went to the window and looked out in time to see a figure at the foot of a ladder. His foreshortened view showed a small bald patch about the size of a pocket watch. The man did not look up and made no attempt to move the ladder, but stepped over a length of lawn, then on to a wide gravel path, and finally into a shrubbery. He disappeared.

There was a rattle of cups, not far away. Cellini moved to the chair in which Maxine Popple had been sitting, and was in it when she entered carrying a tea tray and some biscuits. She glanced round the room in surprise, but made no comment about Selwin. She placed the tray down, carefully, and then asked, 'How is she, doctor?'

'I am waiting for Dr. Selwin to come back before examining her,' said Cellini.

'I thought he would be here,' she remarked, with evident disapproval.

'He went out to try to find the man in the garden,' said Cellini. '*Did* you see him, Mrs. Popple?'

She went pale, but eyed him very steadily. Cellini could see how quickly she might become agitated again, and although she was on edge, there was something fearless in her manner.

'I saw three,' she stated.

'You saw three men in the grounds tonight?' Cellini sounded as if this were wholly unbelievable.

'I saw *three*,' she repeated with gusty emphasis. 'And I've seen them before.'

She stopped, as if defying him to disbelieve her, but he had no thought of disbelief, feeling sure that she was telling the truth; and any doubts he might have had were dissipated by his recollection of the man at the window. He drew the tray a little closer and poured milk into a cup.

'Have you told the police?' he asked.

'No,' she said. 'But I told Popple and he told Mr. Gregory, and *he* said there was no need to worry.'

'Did he explain why?' Cellini began to pour out tea.

She did not answer immediately and he had a sense that she was trying to fight down the temptation to confide in him. He suspected that if he tried to persuade her she would draw back into her shell, and he wanted to know everything she would tell him. He sat back and closed his eyes, sipping.

'Ah,' he said. 'That's a *very* nice cup of tea.' He paused, and then asked what he already knew, 'Has Mr. Gregory run off like this before?'

'Oh, yes,' she said. 'But more's the pity he always comes back.' She clenched her hands in front of her. 'I know I shouldn't talk about the master like this but it's more than flesh and blood can stand, it really is. It's absolutely *wicked*. No woman should have to stand it, she's taken so much.'

'You mean, Mr. Gregory ill-treats *you*?' asked Cellini, deliberately obtuse.

'Oh, not *me*. No, sir, I don't mean me. I mean Miss Melinda.'

Cellini opened his eyes wide.

'A man ill-treats *that* woman?' He glanced at Melinda as if in consternation.

'He never gives her a minute's peace when they're home together,' Mrs. Popple asserted. 'Sometimes I think he hates her so much he wants to drive her mad!' She moved closer to Cellini and lowered her voice until it was on a conspiratorial note. 'Doctor, you are *the* Dr. Cellini, aren't you? The one that's always going into the witness box, I mean, the famous psychiatrist.' Now her eyes were wide open and she seemed to be pleading.

'Yes, I am he,' said Cellini. He sipped tea again, determined not to allow the woman to over-dramatise any aspect of the situation; it was quite dramatic enough in itself.

'Then don't let Mr. Robert pull the wool over your eyes,' warned Mrs. Popple. 'Dr. Selwin's brought you up to see Miss Melinda, but the real pathological case in this house is the master. If he's not mad—'

She broke off, and darted a glance towards the door. For the first time, Cellini heard footsteps; the woman must have ears like a fox. She drew away from him, adding in a whisper which was only just audible, 'I mean it, I'm not exaggerating. He's the one.' Then she turned as Selwin reached the doorway, and asked in a very clear voice, 'Is there anything else you want, sir?'

'Not just now,' Cellini said. 'Thank you.'

The woman went past Selwin and disappeared, taking hardly any notice of him despite the fact that his hair was tousled, his general appearance badly dishevelled, and brown and yellow dried leaves were in his hair and on his shoulders. He took no more notice of the woman than she of him, but as soon as she was out of earshot, he spoke. He was as tense now as Cellini had ever seen him.

'There were three men,' he announced.

'*Three*,' echoed Cellini. 'So Mrs. Popple was right.'

'She was absolutely right. I saw three men leave the front garden, two over the fence and one out of the main gates. They piled into a car and drove off. There wasn't a chance of catching them, I couldn't even get the number of the car. What the devil can be happening?'

'I know how we could find out,' said Cellini.

'How?' Selwin almost barked.

'Consult the police,' stated Cellini.

Selwin did not respond at once, but looked startled, even shaken. It seemed a long time before he shook his head, and then it was very slowly and deliberately.

'No,' he said. 'I wouldn't want to do that.'

'But Jacob, why not?'

'Because if the police came here the Press would follow, and that would lead to scandal which both Bob and Melinda would hate. And—well, Bob has the place watched by private detectives, sometimes he can think only of divorce. So, telling the police is the last thing I would do without consulting him,' Selwin stated flatly.

There was a long pause, and in it Cellini could hear Selwin's rather laboured breathing. Everywhere else there was silence, strange in the sharp brightness of the room. Cellini finished his tea, put the cup down and stood up. He was a head shorter than Selwin and looked very much older, but his back was straight and his shoulders square, and his chin positively thrust itself forward. His expression seemed to startle Selwin, who looked at him blankly.

'A man and a woman have actually fought here, bitterly. The pin-point pupils show that the woman is under morphia. The man has run away. There are three strange men in the grounds who have terrified the staff. My dear Jacob! What has come over you that you have to consult with a patient of questionable mental stability before calling the police. If Robert Gregory is responsible for these night marauders, he should be made to say so.' When Selwin did not answer but stared stubbornly, he went on, 'I shall most certainly consult the police if I am in fact officially consulted by Mr. or Mrs. Gregory. If I am not—Jacob, I am obliged to tell you this: if anything should happen to this couple, I would be duty bound to advise the police of tonight's events, whether I am consulted by the Gregorys or not.'

As he finished, Cellini smoothed his moustache with his thumb and forefinger, and turned towards the door. He was in the passage before Selwin called his name in a husky voice, but he did not stop. He was halfway to the head of the nearer stairs when Selwin came striding after him.

'Manny, don't go.'

'My dear Jacob, what choice have I? It is impossible for me to condone—'

'Why the deuce should you use the word "condone"?'

Cellini said, quite gently, 'Jacob, I don't know what the circumstances are, or what your motivation is, but clearly you should have consulted me or some other psychiatrist a long time before you did. Robert Gregory, according to what I am told, is always distraught, possibly deranged. His wife is under very great emotional pressures. My dear Jacob! Hasn't your handling of the case been—' He paused, and then added, 'at least ill-advised?'

Selwin said harshly, 'I consulted you over two patients. I didn't ask you to come and sit in judgment. I find your attitude offensive.'

'Do you?' asked Cellini softly. 'I am truly sorry.'

He turned away, and this time Selwin made no attempt to call him back. Neither Popple nor his wife were about, and he had to stretch up on tiptoe in order to push back the bolt at the top of the door, but at last the door opened and he stepped out into the chilly night.

No one accosted him.

He got into his old car, which started off with surprisingly little noise, and drove towards the gate. The lights still blazed, and he glided through a cave of radiance. No one was in the street, and in fact he saw no one until he reached the pond. There, two policemen were talking to a little man wearing a suit which was much too large for him.

It was nearly five o'clock when Cellini reached home, and daylight was beginning to show in the eastern skies. He left his car in the forecourt of the apartment block, went upstairs, and slipped quietly into his bedroom. His wife was still asleep, and did not stir. He undressed in the faint light from outside, folded his clothes over the back of a chair, and went back to bed.

He was a long time getting off to sleep, and even when he slept his mind seemed to be haunted by the sleeping beauty, but the hawk-like face of Jacob Selwin was super-imposed on the woman's from time to time. He knew, and he was quite sure that Selwin also knew, there was some-thing gravely wrong in the Gregory household, and that overtones of tragedy hung over it. He hoped, he prayed, that he had not antagonised Selwin too much, for Selwin needed his help almost as much as the other two.

At last, he went to sleep.

He did not know how long he had slept, but when he woke it was broad daylight. His wife was standing by his side, fully dressed, so he had slept late. She had a tea-tray in her hands, and placed it on the bedside table and began to pour.

'Good morning, Felisa,' he said sleepily.

'Good morning, Emmanuel.' She was brisk.

'So it is Emmanuel this morning,' he said teasingly. 'Not Manny.'

'It is Manny only when you behave yourself,' Felisa said. She wore silver grey, tight at the bosom and waist, where she had thickened to stoutness. Her face was the pale yellow of old alabaster, and there was affection in her dark brown eyes. 'To come home at such a time, and not to wake me.'

'How could I wake you when you were snoring so loudly I could not hear myself breathe?' He sat up, smiling at her, looking refreshed and with a pink glow in his cheeks. 'What time is it?'

'Ten o'clock,' she replied.

'*So* late!'

'It is not late for an old man who has been out most of the night,' she rebuked. 'I would not have woken you but for the message.'

He sipped tea which had a perfumed fragrance very

different from the tea which Mrs. Popple had made the previous night.

'Who is the message from?' he asked.

She answered very quietly, 'A Mr. Robert Gregory.'

Cellini started so that he nearly dropped his tea; he steadied the cup, while gaping at her.

'When did it come?' he demanded. 'I mean, the message.'

'It came fifteen minutes ago,' answered Felisa. 'He desires to see you.'

'When? Where?' Cellini almost barked and the sound came strangely from the mild-mannered elderly man. 'What does he want?'

'How can I tell you?'

'*Where is he?*'

'Near by, in Wimbledon.'

'So near this place? Felisa—'

'He will be with you at half-past eleven,' Felisa told him, 'and you have time to bathe while I get your breakfast. Manny, there is no need for you to spring out of bed like a clockwork toy, drink your tea in comfort.'

'Felisa,' Cellini said, 'has anyone else called? I mean, in particular, Jacob Selwin.'

'No,' she answered, to his disappointment.

'There was a newspaper,' Felisa added. 'I said that you were out and would not be back until midday. However, I have the name and telephone number of the young man if you should wish to call back.'

'I wish to call no one back until I have seen Robert Gregory. He really is coming here?'

'He is coming,' Felisa assured him. 'Have no doubt.'

After a pause he wrapped a dressing-gown about his pale but surprisingly muscular body, and went to the window, which was open. It was his practice to stand in front of the open window each morning and to do some deep breathing exercises, without which he seldom felt fully awake.

He drew in a deep breath as he glanced outside, then let the breath out with slow precision.

A dozen men were gathered down there and all were looking towards this or the next-door window. Several had cameras slung over their shoulders. Cellini almost stumbled in his haste to get to one side.

'What is it?' asked Felisa. 'A man of your age, and you are shy.'

'I am not shy,' said Cellini, 'I am shocked. That is, I am shocked if they are waiting for me.'

'They are waiting for you,' she confirmed, and on that instant they saw him.

Almost immediately two men raised their cameras, and one of them used a flashlight. Cellini darted back, but not before he heard a man call out, 'How soon will you be ready, Dr. Cellini?'

And another called, 'Were you at Hethersett last night?'

What did they know and why should they inquire about Hethersett?

'Did you see the man in the grounds?' called a third.

'Felisa, Felisa,' gasped Emmanuel Cellini, 'I do not understand. Why are they here? What has happened? Is—' He caught his breath. 'Is anyone *dead*?'

'No,' his wife answered, serenely. 'But it appears that at this house you visited last night there has been a burglary.' She went on, without even a glimmer of a smile, 'And of course the men from the newspapers wish to know whether you were involved in it.'

She smiled at this great jest, but Cellini did not smile. His agitation fell away from him, and he became very calm. The cloak of dignity which had so impressed Selwin fell upon him again, clad though he was only in pyjamas, barefooted and tousle-haired.

'Manny!' protested Felisa. 'I am joking, only joking!' In her vehemence she made the word sound like 'shoking'. 'They know you were not involved, you can be sure of that.'

Her husband looked at her with a long and searching gaze, then asked in a soft but probing voice, 'What they know or think they know is not important, Felisa. What is important is whether I was involved.'

Felisa looked at him, obviously baffled, and he said nothing to explain that cryptic remark. Soon, he turned back towards the window, and was in time to see a black Rover 3 litre draw up near the group of newspapermen. He recognised the car and pursed his lips when his old friend Superintendent John Hardy of the Criminal Investigation Department of the Metropolitan Police, stepped out of the car into a battery of cameras and, obviously, a battery of questions.

Cellini spun round with almost youthful vigour.

'I must hurry, Felisa, John Hardy is here. Give him coffee if I am not out of the bath when he arrives.' He disappeared into a bathroom which led off the bedroom, while the cameras clicked outside and the questions were fired. She did not look out but hurried to the kitchen. When she began to prepare breakfast the air of bafflement failed, and she became queen of her own domain. When, five minutes later, she opened the door to Superintendent Hardy, she was as smiling and bland as her husband could be.

CHAPTER FIVE

Burglary

Superintendent Hardy was a large, comfortable-looking man with silvery-grey hair and an aristocratic appearance that was nearer the popular conception of a family lawyer than that of a senior police officer. He wore dark horn-rimmed glasses, which added to his air of abstraction and concealed from many the bright and penetrating shrewdness of his blue eyes. When Cellini went into the small dining-annexe of the kitchen, Hardy was sitting back in a rocking chair —Felisa's favourite—drinking coffee which steamed from his cup. He began to get up.

Cellini thrust out a hand.

'Don't get up, John, please.' He drew up a chair for himself and adjusted his dressing-gown, black with an embroidered silver pattern only a shade brighter than his hair. Felisa came in with a coffee percolator and poured him out a cup. 'Good morning,' Cellini added to the detective. 'What brings you round so early?'

Hardy pursed his lips, looked severe, and said, 'It is after eleven o'clock.'

'Oh, dear.' Cellini looked like a small child caught out in some misdemeanour. And he sipped coffee.

'Were you at Robert Gregory's house, Hethersett, last night?' asked Hardy, heavily.

'On an issue of accuracy, I was there in the early hours of this morning.'

'What hours?'

'Between three o'clock and four-thirty.'

'Was everything normal at the house when you left?'

Cellini lowered his coffee cup and studied the policeman very closely. Hardy leaned back in his chair, returning the scrutiny. Small noises of cooking and preparing a tray came from the kitchen, the door of which stood ajar. These two old friends had a deep and natural respect for each other, but they were often on opposite sides of the same fence. Cellini was more often retained by the defence, in a major trial, than by the police, although they consulted him from time to time. Justice, Cellini would say, could only be served if everyone sought the truth. Cellini would be pedantically accurate in all his answers, even on such an unofficial occasion as this.

'The house may have been normal by its own standards,' he answered. 'It certainly wasn't by mine.'

'What was wrong?'

'John,' said Cellini, gently, 'why are you asking these questions?'

'I want the answers before you know why I'm asking them,' replied Hardy, frankly.

'Tell me at least this: is *anyone* dead?'

Hardy answered sharply, 'No. Did you expect someone to die?'

'I expected nothing but the unexpected,' answered Cellini. 'Let me tell you exactly what happened—'

He related the story over a breakfast of hot cakes and maple syrup, bacon and eggs, toast, butter and marmalade, at which he easily out-ate the detective. Hardy listened with the closest attention, without asking any questions, even when Cellini finished a little sadly:

'I know that I should perhaps have sent for you but—' He shrugged his shoulders. 'I did not find it an easy decision, and as I was assured that Gregory often behaved in much the same way, I decided to wait at least until the morning so that he should have a chance to reconsider confiding in me. And also, that I could talk to him about the three men.'

'Who on earth did you think they were?'

'Possibly guards at the house,' Cellini answered. 'Possibly private detectives watching the wife. But I was troubled about them.'

'You weren't troubled enough,' Hardy growled. 'Can you describe them?'

'I saw only one man; Dr. Selwin told me he had seen the others.'

'Ah, yes,' Hardy interrupted. 'Can you describe the one you saw?'

'Yes. He was round-faced, pale, with thin lips; dark eyes, short eyelashes, dark hair with a bald patch on top. Oh, yes—and narrow shoulders, a turtle-neck sweater or shirt and a dark jacket.' Cellini put a piece of buttered toast in his mouth and pushed the toast rack and butter away from him. 'There was a slight familiarity about the features but I cannot recall to whom.'

Hardy laughed.

'The ideal witness!'

'A trained one at all events. What has happened, John?'

'Be prepared for a shock,' warned Hardy, and actually allowed Cellini a moment in which to prepare himself, before adding, 'Everything of value was stolen from Hethersett last night. A pantechnicon was brought into the drive at about half-past four, and at least five men moved the stolen goods out. The whole performance took about an hour and the van left in broad daylight.' Hardy adjusted his glasses, taking them off for a moment and so showing how bright was the blue of his eyes. 'Entry was through the front door. In the excitement, the burglar alarm system had not been switched on, and we shall need to find out whether that was really an oversight. The Popples were locked in their room and Mrs. Gregory was locked in hers. She wasn't harmed in any way. In fact the last I heard she was still unconscious.' Hardy put his glasses back; it was almost as if a light had been switched off. 'The first rough estimate of value, from the insurance company who had a man there by eight o'clock, is three million pounds.'

'Good gracious me!' exclaimed Cellini. He began to play with his knife as he contemplated Hardy, and at last went on, 'Is Robert Gregory at his office?'

'No,' answered Hardy.

'But Selwin said—'

'Selwin was wrong,' interrupted Hardy. 'And you were wrong, Manny.'

'Not to tell you of the man at the window, you mean?'

'Yes, of course.'

'Perhaps,' conceded Cellini. 'I think any procrastination was both understandable and justified, but I could well be wrong. I am much more concerned with another aspect, in which I may be culpable indeed.' He brushed his moustache, aware of Hardy's very hard, questioning expression. 'Was I being used as a distraction, as it were? to distract attention from what was going on outside?' When Hardy didn't answer, he went on, 'I cannot believe that Selwin would connive at such a trick. I am sure he was astounded by the men in the grounds. But Gregory—' He broke off, pursing his lips. 'Gregory could conceivably have staged his performance and even his disappearance in order to distract the others at the house. It is conceivable that he distressed his wife so that she would have to be given a sedative. I—' He snapped his fingers sharply. 'But I am talking nonsense!'

'You're thinking aloud,' said Hardy. 'I've never heard you do that before, nor heard you talk nonsense. Manny, we shall need your help.'

'I cannot see how.'

'We—*I*—want you to see Mrs. Gregory and to talk to Gregory if he returns and find out what you can about them both. From what you've told me there's something very peculiar indeed about the household and its occupants.'

Cellini brooded silently for a few seconds, then answered slowly, 'If I were to do this, of course, the Gregorys and Selwin would have to know that I was acting for the police. I could not act in my professional capacity and then pass on what I learned to you.'

'Be your own judge of how you do it,' conceded Hardy, 'but let me know what you find out about them as individuals.'

'How very discerning you can be, John,' said Cellini. 'There is one thing which I am sure will interest you.'

'What?'

'Robert Gregory is coming here to see me this morning. In fact he was due at half-past eleven! He—goodness! It is now nearly twelve o'clock.' He jumped up. 'Felisa, Felisa! The man Gregory—'

'He is in the sitting-room,' Felisa answered from the door, so promptly that she must have been waiting for the question. 'He came in the back way because he saw so many newspapermen at the front. No,' she answered the unspoken question, 'I did not tell him whom you were with.' She smiled upon Hardy, and withdrew.

Cellini stood up, slowly, frowning and preoccupied, while Hardy watched him intently. There was a long silence before he said:

'I do not want you to eavesdrop, John.'

'I do want to know what he says and you think,' retorted Hardy. 'You have a duty to the police and to society, remember.'

'Yes,' agreed Cellini, rather wearily. 'And I have a duty to my patient.'

'He isn't your patient yet,' argued Hardy.

It was, for Emmanuel Cellini, a strange and unwanted dilemma, and it had crept up on him insidiously, quite without warning. His interest, as always, was the individual human being, although his duty was often to society, to the masses of people whom a single bad human being could harm. He looked at Hardy steadily as he thought, and then spoke much more sharply than before. His diffidence and hesitation seemed to vanish.

'If he needs my help as a doctor,' he said, 'I shall give it. If I can help you as well, I will do so, but make no promise.'

Hardy pursed his lips, and then said resignedly, 'I ought to know better than try to influence you. But remember one thing.'

'Yes?'

'If this comes to trial the prosecution may have to call on you as a witness because you were at Hethersett last night.'

'I am not exactly terrified of the witness box,' Cellini said drily.

He saw Hardy to the door, where Felisa was dusting, obviously so that she could wish the detective good day. Then she looked Cellini up and down, and shook her head sorrowfully.

'I don't know what to do with you. You should have put on a suit for John Hardy, you have no time to change now, Mr. Gregory has waited too long already.' She brushed some crumbs of toast off the lapels of the dressing-gown, then opened the door of the living-room and announced: 'Dr. Cellini.'

Emmanuel Cellini went in as Robert Gregory turned from a glass cabinet set against the middle of the main wall. In this were three ornately wrought gold vases, and their lustre glowed. The sun, shining through the windows opposite the showcase, struck the gold with almost savage brightness, and reflected on Gregory's face; it made his skin look yellow, as if with jaundice. Even when Felisa announced her husband, Gregory looked up slowly and as if with reluctance.

'They are beautiful,' he said, in a tone of reverence.

'They are indeed,' agreed Cellini.

'They are—Cellini vases?'

'Yes,' answered Cellini.

'Was the artist an ancestor of yours?'

'There is said to be a straight descent,' said Cellini, 'but I have doubts about the story's authenticity.' He smiled. 'I am happy enough in the reflected glory.'

'If I were you I would be happy just owning these,' said Gregory.

He drew a deep breath, looked again at the vases and moved reluctantly away. His complexion changed; he had a reddish, florid face, and a coarse skin, especially at the nose. There were some signs of dissipation, but they could also be signs of cardiac weakness, and Cellini was not prepared to form even a private opinion quickly. He shook hands with the man who, like Selwin, was nearly a head taller than he; the palm was cool and the grasp firm.

'I'm sorry I kept you waiting,' apologised Cellini.

'No need to be,' the other assured him. 'Good of you to see me at short notice, anyhow.' He looked Cellini up and down, and began to smile faintly. There was humour and a straightforwardness about the man which Cellini had not expected. 'I suppose I ought to apologise for running out on you last night.'

'Why did you?' asked Cellini, mildly.

'I wanted time to think,' stated Gregory.

'And you needed to be alone in order to think?'

'About this particular subject, yes,' answered Gregory.

'What precisely do you mean by saying that?' asked Cellini. 'Please do sit down.'

'Provided I can sit and look at those vases,' said Gregory, sitting down slowly. He was so intrigued by the vases that he seemed almost to be evading Cellini's eyes.

'Yes, of course.' Cellini sat down opposite Gregory. 'What exactly do you mean, Mr. Gregory?'

Gregory turned away from the Cellini vases, settled back in his chair, and took out a cigarette. Then he glanced round, saw no ashtrays in the room, and played with the case without opening it.

'I had to ask myself whether I am mad, or not.'

'My dear sir—'

'That is really what Jacob Selwin suggested,' went on Gregory, as if there had been no interruption. 'If I need psychiatric treatment then clearly the balance of my mind must be in doubt.' He gave an unexpectedly wide and pleasant smile. 'You won't deny that, will you?'

'I won't deny that a lot of laymen believe that,' replied Cellini. After a moment's pause he went on almost benignly, 'And what decision did you reach? *Are* you mad?'

'I decided that I'm not,' Gregory told him. 'And I also thought it might be a good idea to ask you to prove it. I went off into the country, slept in my car for a few hours, had breakfast at a country inn, and came straight on here.'

That was the moment when Cellini felt a sharp twinge of alarm. He had assumed until this moment that Gregory knew about the burglary, but suddenly he doubted it. And the way the man looked at the vases virtually proved that he had a great love of *objets d'art* and so the loss of all he had in his house would come as a terrible shock.

And it looked as if he, Emmanuel Cellini, would have to break the news to him.

CHAPTER SIX

Shock

Robert Gregory seemed to sense that there was a change in Cellini, and began to frown. He was both handsome and yet in a way repellent, with his short nose and wide, flattened nostrils. There were signs of strain at his eyes and lips, and his lips were cracked, his eyes puffy and red-rimmed. A change came over his expression, a touch of haughtiness which hadn't been there before.

'If I've infringed some professional etiquette,' he began stiffly.

'No. Nothing like that,' said Cellini, and he smiled. 'Please believe me, you are most welcome. However—I have just realised that you are probably unaware of—' He hesitated, deeply troubled; but what could he be but simple and direct? So he added, 'The latest news.'

'News about what?' asked Gregory; he almost barked. Then he cried, 'It's not my wife!'

'No,' Cellini said quickly. 'It may well be as great a shock to her as I'm afraid it will be to you.' His voice was relaxed but he watched Gregory closely as he went on, 'Are you aware of the burglary at your home last night, Mr. Gregory?'

Gregory positively gaped, and after a few seconds echoed hoarsely, 'Burglary?'

'I am afraid so,' said Cellini. 'The newspapermen outside want to interview me because I was at Hethersett, after being consulted by Dr. Selwin, a short time before the burglary.'

He paused, watching closely; at first it did not seem that Gregory understood what he had said, there was bewilderment in his pale blue eyes. He began to breathe heavily, deep lines appearing at his forehead and between his eyes. This could be the onset of a heart attack.

'A burglary,' he repeated.

'A serious one, I'm afraid.'

'How serious?'

'I understand that most of your collection of paintings and other works of art were taken,' said Cellini, as matter-of-factly as he could. 'The police are already investigating, and your insurance company—'

He broke off, for another change, the feared one, was coming over Gregory's face. He was turning colour: first very red, then blue-tinged. Cellini got to his feet quickly.

'Mr. Gregory!'

Gregory gave a gurgling sound in reply.

'Mr. Gregory! Where are your pills?' Now he stood in front of the man, who seemed to be choking. '*Felisa!*' he called in a high-pitched voice, and began to unbutton Gregory's collar. The man was gasping for breath, now and again he choked. And his eyes rolled. Cellini eased him back in his chair and then saw Felisa behind him, raising Gregory's legs to a footstool. Immediately he began to go through the man's pockets. Handkerchief, cigarette case, lighter, comb, wallet—ah! Here was a small bottle. He took it out. About a dozen pale pink tablets were in it, and some written notes on the bottle read: *One tablet to be taken at the onset of an attack. A second may be taken half-an-hour later. If symptoms do not begin to disappear consult a doctor.* He unscrewed the cap as Felisa appeared again, with a glass of water.

Gregory was stretched back in the chair, breathing now through his mouth, blue-purple in the face as he fought for breath. Cellini shook a tablet on to his hand, then dropped it to the back of the man's mouth, and Felisa, who had such a remarkable poise, poured a little water between his lips. He gurgled, swallowed, gulped. Felisa unfastened the laces of his black shoes, Cellini loosened his trousers' waistband. Soon, he was breathing less heavily although it was still painful to watch him.

Cellini moved to a telephone on a corner table, flipped over the pages of a telephone book and in a few moments dialled a Hampstead number. Almost immediately a woman answered.

'Dr. Cellini for Dr. Selwin,' said Cellini. 'Urgent, please.'

'One moment, please.' There was a brief pause before Selwin came on the line. He was even-voiced, and yet Cellini sensed something of the excitement in the way he spoke.

'Hallo, Manny. So you've heard.'

'How sick is Gregory?' interrupted Cellini.

'How *what*?'

'Sick. You prescribed *digitalis* but no strength is on the bottle. Is one tablet really enough?' He paused for a moment and then went on quite sharply, 'Will he be all right if he is made comfortable, or should he be taken to hospital?'

There was hardly a pause before Selwin answered in a completely controlled voice:

'One tablet should be sufficient. If the symptoms haven't cleared in half-an-hour, he may have another tablet. Where is he, Manny?'

Cellini said, 'Thank you, Jacob, thank you,' and rang off.

He turned and looked at the sick man and his own wife but did not immediately move towards them. The tablet was working so well that Gregory's breathing was much better, almost normal, and his colour had improved, too. Felisa, standing by his side, turned to her husband.

'What caused it, Manny?'

'I told him of the burglary.'

'Dear Lord,' she said, and looked with great sympathy at the big man. 'Do you need me any more now?'

'Some coffee will be welcome when he comes round.'

'I shall make some at once,' said Felisa. 'Manny, my cherished one, please sit down. Please rest while you can.' She did not wait to watch him as he sat down but went out. He leaned back in an easy chair, looked at Gregory, and allowed a variety of thoughts to drift through his mind. How the Press would have revelled in this, for instance; and what would have happened if he had been with someone else when he had learned of the burglary. What would Hardy make of his reaction? And Selwin. He, Cellini, had been unnecessarily abrupt and perhaps wrong to pretend he had not heard the last question, but then, he needed time to think. And he did not want Selwin here until he had had a chance to talk to Gregory.

Gregory began to stir.

Ten minutes later he was sitting up, clothes unbuttoned and most dishevelled, yet an imposing figure for all that. He sipped coffee from a cup on a tray at his side. His colour was much better, and although his voice was low-pitched it was clear and firm enough.

'Did you find my pep pills?' he asked.

'Yes.'

'Thank you.'

'It was indeed my pleasure. Mr. Gregory—'

'Yes?'

'I am sorry I had to break such news to you.'

Gregory shrugged.

'Somebody had to, obviously. I'd rather you than the police.'

'Don't you like the police?'

'I don't particularly like the breed, and they'd be full of questions I can't answer. And they always seem to assume guilt even in the most innocent.'

'That has not been my experience,' said Cellini. 'I hope you won't think the same of me! Mr. Gregory—' He paused.

'Yes?'

'Had you been given notice of the burglary?'

'Had I *what*?'

'I assure you that I am asking these questions most objectively,' Cellini told him. 'It is pointless as well as inadvisable to get angry. *Had* you been warned, Mr. Gregory?'

'I—had—not,' answered Gregory with great deliberation. 'I resent the question, and—'

'Mr. Gregory,' interrupted Cellini, 'the police may well wish to ask you much more searching questions than I have any right to ask.'

'You have no right to ask any.'

Cellini contemplated him for a few moments and then inquired:

'Do you wish to consult me, Mr. Gregory?'

'I'm not so sure, now,' Gregory growled.

'But you did give me the impression that you wished to have my professional opinion on certain issues.'

'I told you I wanted your confirmation that I was sane.' Gregory was glowering, but obviously he was making a great effort to restrain himself. He took the bottle out of the ticket pocket where Cellini had replaced it, and went on, 'I damned well know I'm sane.'

'Then why ask for my opinion?'

'I've got my reasons,' rasped Gregory.

'No doubt you have,' said Cellini, coldly. 'I also have reasons for what I do, Mr. Gregory. The man who visited me just now was a senior member of the Metropolitan Police. He asked me to assist the police professionally about last night's burglary. I told him—'

'*You bloody swine!*' roared Gregory, and he began to get up.

'I told him that if I accepted you as a patient I could not

help the police except under the demands of the law. And I asked you if you had had any foreknowledge of last night's burglary for a particular professional reason. If you had said yes, I would not have accepted you as a patient. I would have recommended someone who is not already involved. As you said no, I will gladly accept you, although I think there is one thing I must make clear. If you became my patient and it afterwards proved that you had lied about this foreknowledge I should feel constrained to tell the police anything you said relevant to the burglary.' He paused, after speaking with such precision and dignity, and then went on, 'It is entirely a matter for you to decide whether to consult me, through Dr. Selwin.'

At last, he finished.

It was difficult to judge what the other man was thinking. After his roaring denunciation he had subsided into his chair, sitting erect, eyes narrowed, lips slightly parted. Now, he pursed his lips and thrust his chin forward in an almost simian way. He was silent for a long time, and in the interval Cellini felt weariness dropping upon him. He wished that he had dressed. Why did a dressing-gown make one feel at a disadvantage? His thoughts skipped on; when was this man going to ask about his wife?

At last, Gregory asked, 'If you become my psychiatrist, do you talk to the police?'

'No. Except as I've already told you.'

'So you're an honest man,' Gregory sneered.

'Honesty is comparative,' retorted Cellini blandly. 'I should not betray a client's confidences, and nor would any authority seriously expect me to.'

'All right,' growled Gregory. 'You look like a saint; perhaps you are one.'

'I must tell you now that I do not relish such gratuitous rudeness, Mr. Gregory,' Cellini rebuked with very great dignity. After a short pause he went on, 'And also that if you were wilfully unco-operative as a patient, I could, and most probably would, simply withdraw from the case.'

Gregory stared for a long time, tense at first; then suddenly he laughed. At the same moment he eased himself from his chair and towered over Cellini; looming huge, with his massive shoulders and very thick chest. His jaw would have been thrusting and powerful but for his heavy jowl.

'You could be wrong about that,' he riposted. 'We'll see.' There was another pause and his scowl returned, but obviously this time it was not inspired by Cellini. 'I'd better get home and find out what's been taken. I can hardly believe—' He broke off, distressed, agitated, but more in control of himself. 'Can you smuggle me out the back way? I don't want to be besieged by those bloody coppers before I've been home.'

'I can and will smuggle you out,' Cellini assured him.

'Thanks.' Gregory moved towards the door, and then stopped so suddenly that Cellini banged into him. He did not appear to notice but turned round and asked in a hard voice, 'Is my wife all right?'

'When I last heard she was still under sedation after the night's disturbance,' said Cellini.

Gregory nodded, and stepped into the passage. Felisa appeared for a moment, and Cellini asked:

'Felisa, will you tell the newspapermen that I shall soon see them, at the front?'

As Felisa hurried off, Gregory said drily, 'So that will draw any who are at the back.'

'I trust so,' Cellini said, and led him to the fire escape at the far end of the passage. Soon, he heard him walking heavily down the stairs. This was a four-storey apartment so there wasn't far to go.

Cellini turned back to his own apartment, and went straight to his bedroom. Felisa had laid out a pale grey suit, one of his best, being obviously alive to the probability that he would be much photographed that day. Certainly he could not leave the Press and the photographers outside much longer, although it was difficult to know what to say. As he dressed, he reflected simply that it would merely be a matter of answering their questions, but he should have checked with Hardy about the wisdom of answering them all. He was not very satisfied with himself this morning, and it was not simply because he had had a short night's sleep. It was at least as much because he had an overriding sense of anxiety: a sense that he had been lured into this affair for a purpose. It was no use telling himself that this was absurd. Surely it was too much of a coincidence that on that night of all nights there should have been such a burglary!

As he knotted his pale green tie which matched the socks which Felisa had also put out for him, he looked over the parkland to the sunlit trees, seeing the elderly people and the very young, the dogs chasing or trotting or sniffing. It could hardly be a lovelier day, and he could talk to the Press outside; there was a pleasant garden here and plenty of garden chairs.

'Felisa,' he said, putting his head round the kitchen door, 'I shall go and face these ogres, now.'

'You must tell me all the questions they put to you and how shrewdly you answer each one,' urged Felisa, busily rolling pastry. 'Keep out of the sun, remember,' she warned, raising her voice. 'You won't look so pretty if you are sunburned!'

He was chuckling to himself when he went down in the lift. Three or four men were in the foyer of the building. One of them turned and hurried out while two others focussed cameras on him.

'Just a moment, Dr. Cellini.' Flash.

'Step back a yard, sir, please.' Flash. Flash.

'Just one more, sir.'

By the time they had finished, a crowd was forming, and

Cellini thought a little ruefully of the sunshine outside. But there was no time to suggest that they went out, before the barrage of questions began.

'Were you at Hethersett last night, sir?'

'Do you know the Gregorys well?'

'Who were you attending, Dr. Cellini?'

'Are you officially a consultant to the police, sir?'

'Is Mr. Gregory ill? . . . Or Mrs. Gregory?'

'Were they both at home, sir?'

He answered these and dozens of other questions with a gentle expertise which would have won the fullest approval from John Hardy; and he almost enjoyed the experience. One after another they left, in cars, all pleasant, all obviously pro-Cellini, all obviously looking for gossip and scandal. Their questions about the men in the grounds of Hethersett were little more than perfunctory; apparently the Popples had talked. When the last of them had gone, Cellini went through to the garden, spending ten minutes in the warm sunshine, fascinated by the swooping flight of some house martins. He was still probing in his mind for an answer to the question which perturbed him: why had he been called to Hethersett in the early hours? And was the burglary purely coincidental?

He went out of the garden and into the front drive and parking space as a Jensen car pulled in off the road. It was driven by one man who might—and should—be able to answer at least part of the question.

The man was Dr. Jacob Selwin.

CHAPTER SEVEN

Selwin's Fear

Selwin looked immaculate, tall and eagle-handsome, yet the frown which drew his eyebrows close together gave him an almost forbidding expression. He did not notice Cellini as he walked purposefully towards the front entrance and the self-service lift. He was pressing the bell with obvious impatience when Cellini moved from the bright sunlight into shadow.

'Good morning, Jacob,' he called, and his voice travelled across the square foyer with its beige-coloured walls and outgoing passages. Selwin turned quickly.

'Manny! Is Gregory still here?'

It would be a waste of time to ask how Selwin was so sure that Gregory had been here at all.

'No,' he answered.

'Where has he gone?'

'He told me he was going to Hethersett,' answered Cellini.

At close quarters he could see how tired Selwin was, how red his eyes and how glassy. The lift arrived and the doors opened but he took no notice, gripping Cellini's arm with painful tightness. Cellini would not have dreamed that this man could become so agitated.

'He mustn't see Melinda, do you understand? He mustn't see her.'

'My dear Jacob, why not?'

'She'll try to kill him if he goes there now. She thinks he

is behind the burglary.'

'Jacob, must you dramatise—'

'Oh, you bloody fool,' growled Selwin. 'I'm not dramatis-
ing anything, and sweet reason from Manny Cellini isn't
going to help if they meet face to face this morning.'

'Then why did you leave her alone?' asked Cellini coldly.

'I wanted to see Bob, to warn him. When did he leave
here? Can we stop him? I tell you she'll try to murder him
if he goes home.'

Selwin's voice was quivering, and there could be no doubt
that he believed what he said; and the whys and wherefores
didn't matter. Cellini waved towards the lift. 'Get in,' he
said, and went ahead. The lift went upwards slowly, while
Selwin asked:

'What are you going to do?'

'If you're right, there's only one thing to do,' said Cellini.
'I am going to ask Superintendent Hardy to help.'

'How can he—' began Selwin, but the doors opened and
they stepped out on to the landing. Cellini, now moving with
surprising speed, opened the door of the flat, called, 'It is I,
Felisa!' and picked up a telephone from a small table in the
lobby. He dialled 230-1212 and almost immediately a woman
said:

'Scotland Yard. Can I help you?'

'Mr. John Hardy, please, for Dr. Emmanuel Cellini.'

'One moment.' There was silence at the other end of the
line, but Selwin moved and breathed into Cellini's ear:

'*What are you going to ask him to do?*'

'Sergeant Conway, speaking for Superintendent Hardy,'
said a man with a noticeable north-country accent. 'Who is
that, please?'

'This is Dr. Emmanuel Cellini.'

'Oh, hold on, sir!'

'*What are you going to ask him to do?*' Selwin was gripping Cellini's shoulder even more painfully than before.

'Hallo, Manny,' said Hardy, at last. 'Have you reached your decision yet?'

'John, listen to me,' said Cellini with unmistakable urgency. 'Robert Gregory is on his way to his home. I have good reason to believe that there might be violence if he and his wife meet there this morning. Don't you need to question him?'

'We can't wait to,' admitted Hardy. 'But whose blood is he after?'

'If you will prevent him from going into the house alone, I will tell you all I can afterwards,' said Cellini. 'Don't let him go in by himself, John. It really is important.'

After a pause, Hardy answered gruffly, 'All right. I've men there and I'll tell them to watch him. Goodbye.'

Cellini replaced the receiver and deliberately turned to look at Selwin, whose grip had slowly relaxed. The man's expression had eased somewhat, and his eyes had lost much of their feverish brightness but he looked in desperate need of sleep. He forced a smile.

'I should know I can trust you,' he said.

'I hope I can trust you,' said Cellini, coldly. 'I don't understand you at all.'

Selwin said, 'You don't have to, Manny.'

'I have to,' Cellini insisted, still coldly. 'I need to know, for instance, how it is you can concentrate so much of your time and energy on Robert Gregory, why and how deeply you are involved in this affair, why you are in such need of sleep.' He took Selwin's arm in turn and led him towards his, Cellini's, spare room. 'Have you had breakfast?'

'No, I—'

'Anything to eat or drink this morning?'

'No. A neighbour told my wife about the burglary, and as soon as I heard I rushed over to Hethersett.'

'My wife will prepare a meal for you, and if you want to be even halfway fit for the rest of the day you should loosen your clothes and lie down,' Cellini said, both compassionate and reproving.

Almost petulantly, Selwin protested, 'I am not a child.'

'At times we are all children or at least behave like children,' retorted Cellini, prosily. 'Why don't you take a bath or a shower?'

Selwin dropped heavily on to the side of the bed.

How he had aged, thought Cellini; how pale and drawn he looked. It seemed almost cruel to pressure him, but sooner or later he must explain why he was so involved. Now, Cellini allowed him to relax, with those questions to ponder, and moved to the door.

'Manny,' Selwin said, 'you didn't know I had taken on a partner, did you?'

'No,' admitted Cellini, over his shoulder. 'I had no idea. So he is looking after the rest of your patients.'

'Yes. My conscience is quite clear on that score.'

Something had reassured him; perhaps the full realisation that Robert Gregory and his wife would not be allowed to confront each other by themselves that morning. At all events, Selwin was much more the man whom Cellini knew, and was already taking off his coat. Cellini went away to the kitchen, where Felisa was cracking eggs into a brown bowl.

'I heard you,' she said. 'It is my morning to work in the kitchen! I shall prepare him an omelette.'

'And strong coffee,' suggested Cellini.

'Naturally.'

'Felisa,' went on Cellini, 'you are a jewel. May I ask you, is there a bath towel in the spare room bathroom?'

'Naturally!'

Cellini laughed softly, pleasantly.

'You are a jewel of jewels.' He took a small bottle down from a kitchen cabinet and unscrewed the cap, shaking one tablet into a cup already standing on a tray. 'Will you pour coffee for him? And persuade him to rest for at least an hour. With that tablet I think he will sleep for three hours or four, and I shall be back by then.'

'How is it that you can give a friend drugs?' asked Felisa. 'Have you no shame?'

'Perhaps I have no sense of guilt and therefore no need for shame.'

'Where are you going?' his wife inquired.

'If you do not know you cannot tell Jacob nor anyone who may inquire,' Cellini remarked, almost skittishly. 'I shall telephone you, my jewel.' He kissed her lightly on either cheek, and went out of the room.

Soon he was driving towards the centre of London, and from Marble Arch he headed towards Hampstead. Traffic was intermittently light and heavy, and the whole journey took him less than an hour. The old car attracted attention from a lot of people, especially young men, and admiration sparked in most eyes. He drove alongside the pond where many small children, watched by nursemaids or by mothers, were sailing boats and rafts, bouncing balls and dragging toy animals on strings. It was a delightful day. Soon he turned into the *cul de sac* where Hethersett stood, and was pleasantly surprised to see Hardy's car there. Two plainclothes policemen were in the shrubbery making plaster casts of footprints, and one policeman in uniform stood in the doorway, eyeing the vintage Morris almost in awe. He bestirred himself and opened the door.

'Good afternoon, sir.'

'Good afternoon, and thank you, constable.' Cellini climbed down from the running board. 'Superintendent Hardy is here, I see.'

'Yes, sir, he is. Who—*Oh*!' The man's expression changed comically and with startling suddenness. 'You're Dr. Cellini.'

'I am indeed,' admitted Cellini. 'I have come to see Mrs. Gregory.'

'*Have* you, sir?' A lift of eyebrows could say so much

without a word being said. 'She's up in her room.'

'And the Popples?'

'They're inside, sir. Supposing we press the bell—'

'I don't think we need,' said Cellini, persuasively. 'I know my way about this house.' He gave the constable a disarming, even cherubic smile and went inside. He felt quite daring and a little astonished at himself. He had never before been of a mind to take such a personal part in an inquiry. Naturally punctilious in his behaviour, he yet had a sense of urgency allied to a conviction that he would only find out what he needed to know by taking short cuts. And he needed to know how Melinda Gregory was today.

Suddenly, he stopped in the middle of the hall, alive for the first time to the monstrous nature of the burglary. For the walls were bare. The shelves and recesses where the sculptures had been, were empty. The priceless Persian rugs had gone, only the wall to wall carpet remained. The sofa table against one wall was gone, also two William and Mary chairs, and a dozen small pieces of furniture. A few pictures were left against the blank walls, obviously left deliberately.

'Good gracious *me*!' exclaimed Cellini aloud.

As he spoke, Popple arrived from the passage at one side of the stairs. He looked very pale but much calmer than on the night before. He wore a black jacket, a grey cravat, and striped trousers.

'Good afternoon, sir. Do you—*why*!' His face lit up. 'It's Dr. Cellini!'

'Yes indeed,' said Cellini. 'And how are you, Popple?'

'Everything considered, sir, very well,' replied Popple. 'After the burglary, and what a *terrible* thing that was,' he added in a throbbing voice. 'They couldn't have been here more than two hours and they made a clean sweep of all the really valuable things.' He paused, and switched the subject almost too quickly. 'Afterwards, as I began to say, I was able to get some rest, and as the police were all over the place I had no responsibilities. I will say they were most considerate. After questioning Maxine and me they allowed us to retire. Maxine is with Miss Melinda, sir. Whom did you come to see?'

'Miss Melinda,' Cellini said. 'Why not Mrs.?'

Popple pursed his lips.

Certainly a good long sleep had made a world of difference to him, but something more than that accounted for his changed manner. It was almost as if he had indeed been relieved of a great burden.

'It is a family habit, sir—Americans often seem to say 'Miss'. Soon after she woke Mrs. Popple told her of the burglary and it upset her terribly. I don't really advise seeing her until she has had some rest.' He paused then went on doubtfully, 'Are you very anxious to see her?'

'Very anxious indeed.'

'Well, then, perhaps it will be all right. If you will go up in the lift, sir, I will meet you on the floor above.'

'I am really quite good at climbing stairs,' Cellini boasted.

They walked together, and on the walls of the staircase, on either side, along the passages, there were the blank spaces where furniture and pictures had been. Once, Cellini stepped on a bare board.

'There was a beautiful Mirzapore rug there, sir,' Popple reminded him. 'They really did take everything of value, it was almost as if they had visited the house and taken notes of all that was worthwhile. It was a terrible thing.' But Popple sounded almost light-hearted, keyed-up perhaps by the excitement. 'Although to tell you the truth in a way it is almost a relief to Mrs. Popple and me.'

'Really?' asked Cellini, sounding as intrigued as he felt.

'There's been something wrong, sir—these men in the grounds from time to time, it was almost as if they were intent on scaring everyone out of their wits. In fact they did scare Mrs. Popple and me! Now I feel it's all over. They were obviously doing what I believe the Americans call "casing the joint".'

Cellini nearly snorted at the phrase coming from prim Popple.

'And is Mrs. Popple also much relieved?'

'She is indeed, sir. And here is the suite.'

They stopped outside a closed door, through which the sound of music came faintly. Popple opened this and the music sounded much more loudly. His wife was sitting with some mending in her lap, nodding her head to the beat of the instruments as the orchestra played one of the waltzes from the Vienna Woods. This came through a doorway which was partly open. Mrs. Popple had the same rested look as her husband, and the lilting tune did not suggest any mood of violence in the woman in the other room.

'Why, doctor!' Mrs. Popple exclaimed, getting up with surprising agility. 'I didn't expect you.'

'I want to have a talk with—' began Cellini, but he stopped short, for Melinda Gregory appeared in the doorway at that moment.

His first impression was of her astonishing beauty; his second, of the simple perfection of the lilac-coloured dress she wore; his third, of the glare which suddenly appeared in her eyes.

'Who are you?' she demanded.

'I am Dr. Cellini, and—'

'Get out,' she ordered. 'At once.'

'I hope, Mrs. Gregory, that you will spare me a few minutes. I really will not detain you for very long.'

'You won't detain me at all,' she answered icily. 'Popple, show this man out.'

Popple on one side, Maxine on the other, were obviously greatly embarrassed, but Melinda Gregory's manner was imperiously demanding, and clearly Popple had no choice but to obey. But before he moved or spoke, Manny Cellini

looked up at the angry woman, then said with equal coldness, 'You are a very foolish woman, Mrs. Gregory, as well
as a very rude one. And it is a great pity to see such beauty
spoiled.'

He turned on his heel, heard a rustle of movement and a
stifled cry from Maxine, and then felt a heavy blow on the
side of the head. Although half-prepared, he went stumbling,
as it happened, into Popple.

'Madame!' Popple cried. 'Madame, please!'

Cellini recovered his balance, while Melinda raised her
hand as if to strike him again. Where most men would have
backed out of reach of this woman who had suddenly become
a virago, Cellini went forward, evaded her blow, and gripped
her wrists. She caught her breath and stood staring—glaring
—at him.

CHAPTER EIGHT

Melinda

Cellini maintained his grip only for a few seconds longer, then released Melinda. He half-expected her to strike again but something in his manner or in his gaze restrained her. He lowered his hand to his side, and for a second time, turned away. There was no blow and no sound to suggest that she was following him. Popple looked almost as upset as he had the previous night; his release from tension might prove to be wholly superficial. Mrs. Popple sat very still, her chair rocking slightly.

Cellini reached the door.

'What is it you want?' Melinda called, hoarsely.

'A talk with you about your husband,' answered Cellini.

'I'm not interested in my husband.' Venom was in her voice.

'So I understand.' Cellini turned to face her and was astonished afresh by her beauty and the clarity of her skin. 'However, he may be in need of help.'

'Then let him look to someone else for his help.'

'He has: he has looked to me.'

'And he's sent you crawling to me,' she sneered. 'Let me tell you, Dr. Whoever you are, if I ever get the chance I will kill him. Do you understand me? I'll kill him.'

'I have little doubt that you would try,' said Cellini coldly. 'As I said before, you are a very foolish woman. If you killed or attempted to kill your husband you would spend much of the rest of your life in prison. Is that what you want? The wholly celibate, wholly unnatural life of a prison cell?'

She frowned, as if he baffled her; and then she glanced quickly from one Popple to the other, and said imperiously, 'You may go.' She turned and led Cellini into the inner room, and it was almost possible to hear what Popple was thinking: *be careful, sir*. But the Popples moved into the passage and closed the door, while Cellini went into the room where he had seen Melinda, then a sleeping beauty, last night.

This was a lovely room and nothing had been disturbed. The bed was on one side, made, and obviously unused during the day. A record player, now mute, stood by the window, and there was a beautifully quilted sofa with a table by the side, a box of chocolates and what looked like a jar of ginger on it. The jar looked very old. Through the window Cellini caught glimpses of men in the garden: the whole place had been taken over.

'*He* did that,' she said, venomously.

'Who did what?' asked Cellini.

'My precious husband organised the burglary.'

'Oh.' Cellini smiled at her mildly. 'Have you told the police yet?'

'Why should I help them do their job?'

'To help them to recover the stolen goods,' replied Cellini, patiently.

'They haven't a hope in a million!'

'They won't even have that if you don't tell them what you know. Mrs. Gregory—'

'Dr. Cellini,' Melinda Gregory interrupted, 'aren't you a little old to expect a woman to be rational?'

Now, at least, she was half-smiling, and he wasn't sure whether it was at him or at some reflection in her mind. He was momentarily nonplussed, and it did not seem a bad thing that she should enjoy a moment of triumph. At last, he retorted, 'I am not too old to hope even for miracles, my dear.'

At that, she laughed naturally, and moved to the sofa. She walked gracefully, sank into it gracefully, and motioned to a chair between it and the window. Her lovers' seat? he wondered. She picked up the box of chocolates and proffered it. He selected one with great care, in anticipatory enjoyment, said 'thank you' and popped it into his mouth. Then with admiration which he did not have to fake, he went on, 'You act so beautifully, Mrs. Gregory.'

She looked at him straight-faced, and echoed: '*Act?*'

'My dear lady, you don't really expect me to believe that you lost your self-control just now.'

She put a chocolate into her mouth, and laughed with obvious enjoyment.

'No, I didn't,' she admitted.

'So you struck me quite cold-bloodedly.'

'Do you expect me to say I'm sorry?' Her eyes were brimming over with laughter. She hardly seemed the same woman.

'Not unless you feel sorry,' he said.

'I think I could feel sorry, with you.'

'Please wait until you are certain!' Cellini's eyes gleamed, and he paused before going on in the same even tone, 'Why do you hate your husband so?'

'Because he is a hateful creature.'

'Not everyone would agree with you.'

'Nobody has to, he is perfectly nice to them. He is hateful to me. In fact, Dr. Cellini,' she went on, leaning forward intently, 'if I were to tell you *all* the reasons why I hate and abominate the man to whom I am married it would shock you.'

'I doubt it,' said Cellini drily.

'I would prefer not to put it to the test,' she retorted.

He contemplated her for a few moments in silence, and during this she proffered him another chocolate; he selected one with the same care as before, and ate it with equal relish.

'Thank you. So you think your husband staged this robbery himself?'

'*He* lost nothing,' she declared.

'I beg your pardon?' Cellini was startled.

'Everything here was really mine,' she said, flatly. 'Everything. My husband didn't own a penny piece in this house. He mortgaged everything to raise capital for his business, and he is in desperate need of more. *I* redeemed the mortgages.' She leaned forward and looked very closely into Cellini's eyes. 'Unfortunately I forgot one little formality. I forgot to have the insurance put into my name. So, he will claim the insurance.' She drew in a sharp breath and her eyes glittered, she practically spat as she demanded, 'Wouldn't *you* want to kill a husband who did that to you?'

Slowly, Cellini answered, 'I can understand the temptation, at all events.'

'Dr. Cellini,' said Melinda with great deliberation, 'I am a woman of my word. And I warn you that sooner or later I shall kill Robert Gregory. I shall kill him with my own hands. When you see him, tell him so for me, will you?'

Almost at once, Cellini answered, 'I will certainly tell him.'

She nodded, as if satisfied, and told him quietly, 'I'm staying up here until the police have finished with him, and then I want him to be thrown out. The house is mine, too, and I don't want him in it for another moment. *Do* you regard him as a patient?' she asked quickly.

'Yes,' he answered.

'Did he send you to see me?'

'No.'

'Then it must have been Jacob, who—'

'I came entirely of my own free will,' Cellini interrupted, 'and without the knowledge of either of them. You see—' his smile was quite charming—'I had seen you last night and you were so beautiful that I had to see what you were like when you were awake.'

'How very gallant,' Melinda mocked. 'Do you know, Dr. Cellini, I believe you could be quite a wolf if you were to let yourself go.'

'Don't you mean I could have been?' asked Cellini wickedly.

'No,' she answered, her eyes glowing. 'I don't think age has much to do with wolves. Or if you don't mind me being forthright, with sex. I have known—' She broke off, without the slightest warning, as if something had suddenly caught in her throat, and then very slowly her expression and her manner began to change.

Cellini watched, fascinated.

He had been quite sure when he had first seen her that she had been pretending fury, but now he thought she was truly becoming enraged. Her lips tightened, her eyes narrowed and yet glinted, and in a peculiar way her breathing grew short and shallow. A vein ridged out at the side of her neck like a piece of whipcord against that lovely skin.

She said evenly, 'You unspeakable swine. You come here with your filthy questions and you're working for him. You've come to try to prove that I'm mad. Get out.'

'My dear Mrs. Gregory—' Cellini protested.

'Get out, or I'll send for the police to throw you out! And tell your client if he ever comes near me again I'll cut his throat.'

Cellini answered very quietly, 'Very well, Mrs. Gregory, I will leave. Will you answer me just one question? A very personal question. Remember I *am* a doctor and I have the interests of all people at heart.'

'You are a cold-blooded liar,' she accused.

'I am a doctor of psychiatry attempting to help his patients in most trying circumstances,' said Cellini. 'Will you answer that question?'

After a long pause, she said, 'Try me.'

'Very well. Why do you have so many lovers?' While she looked astounded but did not respond, he went on, 'Is it because you are miserable and unhappy, or is it because you enjoy the pleasures of the flesh in infinite variety?'

When he finished, the room was still with an almost deadly hush. Her face paled but nothing else changed, except that the vein began to pulse until it almost mesmerised him. Soon, he began to realise that he had shocked her out of the mood she had been in only a moment or two before.

'Lovers,' she echoed, in a sighing voice.

'Yes,' said Cellini.

'Oh, you fool,' she said, 'Oh, you fool.' Then she gave a short bark of a laugh, and went on, 'Would you expect any woman to tell you that? Would you?'

'Not any woman,' Cellini answered. 'But you—yes.'

She turned away and looked out of the window, and now a vein in the back of her neck stood out, as if she were losing her self-control again, but she spoke quite freely although in a hard voice.

'I have never met a man worthy of being my lover.'

'Yet it is said you take many lovers,' Cellini remarked, gently.

Her head moved. She raised her hands to it and buried her fingers in her hair, and then her shoulders moved and she began to laugh. The laughter grew louder, a paroxysm so violent that it held a hysterical note. He began to feel alarmed. She actually tugged at her hair as if to make her head go to and fro and she laughed and laughed until the sound was hideous. His alarm grew. She was near hysteria, perhaps already in the grip of it. He moved forward quickly, faced her, and said sharply:

'Stop laughing, *now*.'

But she went on laughing. Her head was back and her mouth wide open, showing her beautiful teeth. Her stance thrust her bosom provocatively against her dress and emphasised the slenderness of her waist. Her eyes were nearly closed, tears were beginning to fall from them.

Cellini moved, and slapped her across the face. It had no effect at all. He slapped again with even greater vigour and this time made her pause, but she continued to laugh and her whole body quivered.

If he could not quieten her, he would have to call the Popples.

'Mrs. Gregory,' he said sharply, 'stop this absurd behaviour. At once!'

And, to his relief but astonishment, she stopped. She stared for a few moments and then, when he thought she was really over the paroxysm, she moved forward and took his wrists and drew him close with a sudden movement of unexpected force.

'*You* be my lover,' she whispered. 'You show me what a masterful male you are beneath that silvery hair and that beautiful silvery moustache. Prove yourself a *man*.' She held him very close, and in one way this could not be more humiliating, but in a way it could not have been more revealing. 'Come on, great lover,' she whispered hoarsely. 'Here we are, just you and I and a big, big, beautiful bed!'

He could feel her heart beating as she pressed his head close to her. He could feel the yielding softness of her body, for beneath the dress she wore so little, perhaps nothing but a brassière and panties. He was trapped, momentarily, and could not free himself without hurting her and he did not want to hurt her more than he must. He was acutely, uncomfortably, aware of the undulations of her body. Her arms rose, and it seemed only a split second before her dress was slipping off her shoulders, a moment more before she had unhooked her brassière and let it fall.

'Come on, lover,' she whispered. 'Prove what a man you are.'

* * *

Her body was as beautiful as her face, Cellini saw.

It was more than 'seeing', it was knowing; being acutely aware; being almost obsessed, as she flaunted her body before him.

He was aware of her glowing womanhood.

And he was aware of himself, as a man, as he had not been in many years.

She was smiling at him, luring him, seducing him.

She was on the bed, beautiful, waiting for him.

'Come,' she whispered, 'come and make love to me. Come and love me. If you can excite me then you are indeed a man—

'Come, Cellini.'

'Come.'

* * *

When he did not move but stood transfixed, affected as he had seldom been even in his early manhood, she held her hands out, arms widespread, in a gesture so sensuous and so sexual that he felt the blood rush to his head and to the physical male in him.

'No one need know,' she whispered. 'Have you a wife? She need never know. And my husband. He will never know, he never dares to come into this room, now. You are quite safe. And I promise you ecstasy such as you have never known. *Come*, my darling, come to me.'

* * *

No one need ever know.

He, Manny Cellini, actually repeated those words to him-

self, and was so sorely tempted that he could not move away.
But he had to. He must not go forward and touch her, or
he would be lost, and in a way, destroyed. It was almost as
if he had been brought here so that he *could* be destroyed.
The blood droned in his ears and coursed through his body.
She was like a magnet; no, a siren: smiling, beckoning, calling, offering herself. He knew that he must not take her and
yet he did not know how to turn away.

But he must.

He must find a way of unlocking the prison into which
his body had been forced, and his mind and his blood. He
must not wait for others to come: good heavens, what
would happen if the door opened now and someone burst
in? Now the veins stood out on his forehead and neck.

He must find a way of refusing her without destroying her
pride in her body.

He must *speak*.

He moistened his dry lips, and spoke in a voice so
husky that he hardly recognised it as his own.

'Melinda,' he said, 'you are the most beautiful woman
with the most beautiful body I have ever seen. But I am a
doctor, and I must not yield, however great the temptation.
Also I have appointments now—including one with your
husband. I really have to go.'

She looked at him hard-faced, the glitter back in her eyes.
The sensuous, seductive woman had changed; there was no
softness in her voice or her expression.

'If you help him,' she said, 'I'll kill you, too.'

CHAPTER NINE

Puzzled Policeman

Superintendent John Hardy watched Robert Gregory go out of the room where they had talked for the past hour. The room of lovely proportions was stripped almost bare. From it alone, if the evidence was right, over three million pounds in paintings and antiques had been stolen. A Vermeer, a Rubens, a Van Gogh and a Utrillo were among the paintings gone, a Turkish carpet officially valued at ten thousand pounds had been taken up, two early English coffers and a cabinet full of gold and jewelled regalia was missing. From the bookshelves, a first edition Shakespeare folio had been taken; the variety was legion and the value almost beyond Hardy's conception.

The door closed on Gregory's rumpled jacket and tousled hair. He hadn't shaved, and obviously hadn't slept. What would he do now? When he had first arrived the manservant Popple had pleaded with him not to go to his wife's quarters. The evidence of the burglary had calmed his emotions down to a cold anger, even Hardy's questions—obviously implying that he, Gregory, might be a party to it—scarcely ruffled his composure.

The check-list was not yet complete, and policemen and insurance assessors were working together from the catalogue and index, but the total loss was now officially known to be worth over the original estimate of three million pounds.

Hardy, not an envious man, and comfortably off by this

world's standards, felt a flash of resentment. Why should any man and woman have the right to such possessions when so many people even in England were on the borderline of hunger and poverty?

The flash faded. He was a policeman, he had to be objective; whether a man was a millionaire or a pauper he had equal rights and equal claims on the law. He got up from a bow-fronted Queen Anne desk, one of the few pieces of value left in the room, and crossed to the window.

Gregory was getting into his car.

'Not going to face that shrew upstairs, sir,' remarked Detective Inspector Percival, who came in on that instant; he had preceded Gregory out of the room. 'What a household!'

Hardy turned and looked at Percival thoughtfully. He was a tall, lean, sharp-featured man with eyes that were oddly deep-set beneath a broad, smooth forehead. He kept his hair cut very short, perhaps to increase the appearance of oddness. There was no doubt that he could make a lot of people nervous under questioning. In contrast to Gregory he was dressed immaculately and he was smiling so broadly it was almost a grin.

'Who told you Mrs. Gregory was a shrew?' Hardy asked, a note of reproof very evident in his tone.

'Well, from what one hears— ' began Percival, in self-vindication, but he stopped abruptly and his smile faded. 'I'm sorry, sir. I shouldn't have said that.'

'That kind of thinking, let alone that kind of talking, could create a prejudiced attitude we can't afford,' Hardy said, less coldly. 'Did he say where he was going?'

'To his club and then his office, sir.'

'Who've we got working on the business angle?'

'Evans went over to the City Police, sir, to check on Gregory's business activities.'

'Call Evans and tell him I'd like to see him as soon as I'm back at the Yard.'

'Right, sir. Oh—one thing.'

'What?'

'Manny Cellini's here.'

Hardy forced back a flash of irritation with this man, whom he knew to be a better-than-average detective. Of course the whole of the Metropolitan Police Force knew Cellini as 'Manny' but coming from Percival it was an over-familiarity, in keeping with other indications that he was getting above himself. Percival was oblivious of the mood, and was back to his near-grin.

'Where is Dr. Cellini?' asked Hardy.

'Up in my lady's room.'

'How long has he been here?'

'About three quarters of an hour. Tell you another thing—'

'Percival,' interrupted Hardy, 'you're in a very chummy mood this morning and I don't know that I like it.' He paused long enough for his rebuke to register, and for a mask of concealment to spread over Percival's face, before going on, 'What else is there to report?'

Percival, standing very erect, said formally, 'Apparently there was some shouting when he went to see Mrs. Gregory. She was heard to tell the manservant to throw Dr. Cellini out.'

'Was she, then! But Dr. Cellini survived.'

'Apparently, sir.'

'I'd expect no less,' said Hardy, smiling faintly. 'All right, I'll see him before he leaves, but don't hurry him. Get that message through to Evans, say I'll be at the Yard by five o'clock at the latest, and then check the missing list until we know we've got everything down. As soon as we have, make the list a hand-out to the Press. How many are outside?'

'Not many now, sir—half-a-dozen or so.'

'Then they can have the list first,' said Hardy, and nodded dismissal.

Percival went out, leaving Hardy with a few minutes, at least, on his own. He welcomed the respite. Only yesterday he had finished an inquiry into the murder of a Hatton Garden jeweller, and he could have done with a week without an assignment, but had been called at his bachelor flat in the Adelphi, London, to be alerted to this one.

'And check with the City over Gregory's firm, *Gregory and Wolf*,' the Assistant Commissioner had urged. The A.C., no doubt, had been speaking from the telephone at his bedside early that morning.

When there was a major robbery, such as this, some possibilities immediately spoke for themselves. This could be an insurance fraud, and if Gregory's bank was in any kind of trouble, this could be a motive for such a fraud. Hardy had found Percival to be the best man available as his aide. He had told him to start the inquiries in the City of London—inquiries which had to be made in co-operation with and under the auspices of the City of London police, who were autonomous in their small but extremely important business section of London—and then gone to see Cellini.

Hardy had come 'cold' into the situation, although knowledge of Cellini's presence here had forewarned him that someone at the house was in need of psychiatric treatment. So he had been half-prepared for emotional outbursts and scenes. He had not come prepared to find Gregory missing and the woman, fresh from induced sleep, hysterical one moment and cold as ice the next. His morning talk with Cellini had helped to clarify the situation in one way and confuse it in another. Manny Cellini was seldom in any way confused but he certainly had been over this.

There was a tap at the door.

'Come in,' called Hardy, and Percival put his head round the door, obviously having taken his rebuke to heart.

'Dr. Cellini's on his way down, sir.'

'Thanks,' said Hardy, and got up.

As he went into the hall, Cellini was coming down the main staircase, and Hardy was immediately struck by a marked difference in him. He seemed a little—*dazed*. As usual he was beautifully dressed and startlingly attractive-looking with his plentiful silver hair and big silver-coloured moustache; Felisa always made sure he was at his best. Often, too, he looked thoughtful and preoccupied, but this would clear the moment he had to speak to anyone, or the subject was changed.

Now, he looked quite blankly at Hardy.

It was a remarkable moment. Percival stood still, staring at Cellini as if the difference startled him, too. Two other detectives, one a photographer, also stood and watched. Cellini came down the wide stairs slowly, without touching or even going near the banister rail; it was as if he were in a trance.

He stopped, a few stairs up. He seemed to shake himself and in so doing shake the mood off. He smiled, vaguely at first and then in recognition at Hardy, and the spell was broken.

'Hallo, John,' he said. 'I hoped you would still be here.' He looked round at the men who immediately resumed their tasks. 'I am always fascinated by the rigours of police routine. Dare I ask: have you discovered anything which might lead to the recovery of the stolen art works?'

'We haven't had much time yet,' Hardy replied.

'Nor, obviously, much luck,' said Cellini, which proved that his mind was as alert as ever. He followed Hardy into the big, bare room, where apparently the fierce quarrel between the Gregorys had started last night, and soon they were ensconced in large and comfortable armchairs.

'Well, Manny,' said Hardy. 'What's hit you?'

Cellini gave a little smile, a smile of a chastened cherub.

'You would never believe me,' he said. '*I* can hardly believe it,' he added, and looked as if he were utterly baffled. 'I'm not even sure I should tell you.' He leaned back and crossed his hands over his stomach, half-concealing the gold of a watch chain.

'I've never known you in such a tantalising mood,' remarked Hardy.

'It is a long time since I have been in one. When has an attempt last been made by a beautiful woman to seduce *you*, John?'

Hardy began, 'What—' He swallowed the word, his mouth falling open. 'You mean Mrs. Gregory attempted to seduce *you*?'

'Yes.'

'Good God!'

'I was somewhat surprised myself,' confessed Cellini. 'And even to a degree flattered. However, I can hardly believe that the lady was so taken by my charms that she immediately became compliant, even persuasive, so there must have been a reason. She presumably wanted to lure me away from her husband. Don't you think that was a very peculiar way of doing it?'

'*Peculiar*,' echoed Hardy. 'I—'

He broke off again, his eyes astonished and incredulous as they observed Cellini, smiling now, as a cat after a succulent meal or a saucer of creamy milk. When he unlaced his hands and smoothed his moustache with his thumb and forefinger, Cellini's expression was one of replete satisfaction. And as he watched, curiosity grew in John Hardy: awareness of a possibility so unbelievable that at first he pushed it out of his mind; but it returned and his desire to know the truth became so overwhelming and compulsive that he could not repress a question which seemed to phrase itself.

'Manny,' he said almost inaudibly, 'you didn't, did you?

I mean—' He broke off, and groaned, 'Oh, I'm sorry. I—
Goddammit, I'm sorry.'

'John,' said Cellini, in a tone of gentle reproof, 'my honour
is unsullied, if that is what you want to know.'

'*Your* honour,' ejaculated Hardy.

'Mine,' affirmed Cellini. 'Despite quite remarkable provocation, inducement and opportunity, I remained loyal to my
professional code and faithful to my Felisa. Not that Felisa—'
He stopped himself and sat up straight. 'Well, never mind.'
An almost seraphic smile now stole across his face, and he
went on, 'I can tell you that Mrs. Gregory is a very beautiful
woman.'

'What the devil went on up there?' demanded Hardy, his
voice only a little stronger.

'Do you know I'm not yet sure, but I would dearly love
to find out,' answered Cellini. 'In fact I am quite determined
to find out. But I am in something of a quandary, John.'
When Hardy simply watched and waited, he went on in
an apologetic tone, 'Gregory would like to consult me with
the object of proving that he is sane. Presumably his wife
would like me to prove that he is a master criminal who
organised last night's burglary. And I understand that the
police would officially like to consult me in their inquiries.
Or have you changed your mind?'

'No,' replied Hardy, faintly. 'We haven't changed our
minds.' He pursed his lips. 'At least I can see your quandary.'

'I am sure you can. And I need a little more time in which
to resolve it,' went on Cellini. 'I need to consult Felisa,
I really do. She'—he gave a funny little laugh—'she will
revel in the situation.'

'You mean you'll *tell* her—' began Hardy, and gave up.

'Most certainly I shall tell her. What is marriage for if it
is not for the sharing of experiences and the mutual enjoyment of each other's excitements?' He contemplated Hardy
quizzically before going on, 'For a bachelor, John, you have

the most conventional of attitudes. One day I must talk to you about my philosophy of marriage but I doubt this is the time. There is one thing I would like to ask you.'

'Go ahead,' said Hardy. And then with a rush, 'If you mean will I keep all this to myself, of course, I will.'

'John, John, I would not even begin to think you would betray such a confidence,' Cellini assured him. 'No, I really want your unofficial view of the situation. If I cannot honestly accept your invitation to co-operate at all levels, yet continue to work in the interests of the Gregorys, can I hope to receive information from you from time to time?'

'About the progress of the case?' asked Hardy.

'What else, my friend?'

Hardy pondered, pursed his lips, and then replied almost prosily.

'Obviously I can't give you official information, but I can often give you items ahead of the Press. I never have refused to, have I?'

'No. No indeed. But this case being so unusual—' Cellini broke off, and rose from his chair with a briskness very different from his manner when he had first come into the room. The dazedness, the complacency, had faded. He was bright-eyed, his cheeks glowed, there was unfamiliar vigour in his movements. 'John, thank you. And of course I will give you any help I can, but you already know that.' He raised his eyebrows as if struck by a new, and amusing idea. 'Have you seen Melinda Gregory yet?'

'No.'

'Then, my friend, be advised by me and be very, very, careful!'

They stared at each other in silence for a few seconds, and then suddenly began to laugh together.

CHAPTER TEN

Defiant Lady

Soon after Cellini had driven off, photographed by two newspapermen and a small boy, Hardy called for the reports of the case so far available. He sifted through them and came upon the one on Melinda Gregory, containing a photograph which Percival had placed in the folder. A study of her picture, in colour, made Hardy purse his lips, then smile in recollection of Cellini's story. He ran through the statement.

First: Dr. Jacob Selwin had testified that he had given her an injection of morphine at twelve thirty the previous night. He had expected this to make her 'sleep' for at least eight hours. And it had.

Second: Benjamin Popple and Maxine Popple had testified that they had seen her asleep as late as eleven thirty that morning.

Third: Percival himself stated that he had interviewed her at two fifteen, and remarked: 'She was brusque and ill-mannered until told of the robbery, when she went into hysterics, and abused the servants, the police and her husband.' Percival had added: 'There appears no reasonable doubt that she was under sedation during the period of the burglary and for several hours thereafter.'

The perfect alibi, mused Hardy.

He looked for the report on Gregory and found nothing of interest until Cellini had told of his visit.

The Popples, according to Chief Inspector Percival, had

been asleep during the period of the burglary. And: 'Popple appeared bewildered and shocked, but recovered and behaved calmly. His wife, Maxine, appeared mostly concerned with what Miss Melinda would say.'

Hardy finished reading, and then vacillated between interviewing Melinda Gregory and waiting until the morning. Suddenly, he laughed at himself: Cellini had almost persuaded him that it would be unsafe to see her! He sent word by a sergeant that he would like her to come down to the big room. Five minutes later, the sergeant, named Carpenter, came back alone.

'Well?' said Hardy.

'She—er—she said if you wanted to see her you could go upstairs.' Carpenter was obviously a little shaken.

'And?' urged Hardy.

'She said she wouldn't come downstairs if you were the Home Secretary himself.'

'She wasn't very gracious, I suspect,' said Hardy.

'She was pretty blunt, sir.'

'Foul-mouthed?' inquired Hardy.

'No, sir. But she's got a pretty fair vocabulary.' Carpenter was in his forties, an amiable-looking man with good features, fair hair which grew far back from his forehead, and a heavy chin. He went on almost apologetically: 'Haven't had a tongue-bashing like that since I joined the Force, sir.'

'H'mm,' said Hardy. 'I'll go and see her. Come with me.'

'Right, sir!' Carpenter agreed in a manner which seemed to say, 'This will be something to see.'

Hardy was aware of many covert glances from his men, who had obviously heard about the 'tongue-bashing'. He went up the bare staircase, only half-aware of how much furniture was missing, also that the police would probably need to stay for another whole day, possibly for two. Men were taking photographs and measurements all over the place, and at least three insurance assessors were present. Coming to the main landing, Hardy saw a tall, very thin man from *Fingerprints*, coming out of a room which seemed to have only a bed in it.

'Hullo, Miller,' said Hardy. 'What can you tell me?'

'Not a fingerprint from anyone outside of the household excepting Dr. Selwin,' answered Miller. 'This is the last room, sir. And I just finished a second check on the front door, with Inspector Webb.'

'And what did you find?'

'Plenty of jemmy marks but not a single print. It was an expert job all right, but it couldn't have been done if the burglar alarm had been on. It's a foolproof system.'

'Who usually switches it on?'

'Mr. Gregory or Mrs. Gregory, sir.'

Hardy nodded, and walked on with Carpenter until Carpenter said, 'Next door on the right, sir. There's a dressing-room and the bedroom's beyond.'

Hardy nodded, reached the door, and knocked; there was no answer. He knocked again, still without an answer. He turned, nonplussed, to face Carpenter, who seemed startled. Hardy tried the handle of the door, but it was locked.

'Her way of saying that she doesn't want to be bothered,' suggested Carpenter uneasily. 'She really is a—' He broke off. 'She certainly knows her own mind, I mean.'

'Yes, I know,' said Hardy, grimly. He clenched his fist and banged heavily on the door, then called, 'This is Superintendent Hardy. Open the door, please.'

There was no response at all.

Carpenter, who had never known the great Hardy flouted in such a way, looked awkward. Hardy was torn between making a lot more noise, and sending for the servants. There was a possibility of course, that Melinda Gregory had left her rooms but this was much more likely to be an act of defiance. He studied the lock, and then pressed hard at the top and bottom of the door; it yielded slightly. He stood back.

'All right,' he said. 'Get a couple of hefty chaps, and have the door down.'

'*Down*, sir?'

'Yes. Get a move on,' Hardy urged.

Carpenter hurried to the staircase and Hardy heard him call, 'Jones! Smithson! Come up.' Soon, the two massive men were hurrying along this passage, and Carpenter had obviously briefed them. They began as if this were a familiar drill, measured themselves against the door, then one put his shoulder against it while holding the handle, and the other drew back to hurl himself against it. '*Now*,' the man at the door ordered, and threw his whole weight against the door while the other pushed and twisted the handle. There was a heavy thump and a creaking noise. The men drew back, and repeated the onslaught. '*Now!*' the thudding and creaking was much louder, and the door sagged.

Then from inside the room a woman screamed, '*Stop that! Stop it!*'

The two men stood aside, and Hardy called out, 'Is that Mrs. Gregory?'

'Of course I'm Mrs. Gregory! What the hell do you mean by—'

'Open this door, at once.'

'I don't intend—'

'Open this door in the name of the law,' called Hardy in a firm voice.

'Oh, go to hell!'

'Mrs. Gregory,' Hardy called, 'if you don't open this door at once I shall have to break it down. The choice is yours.' He did not add that if he allowed her to stay locked in, and she committed suicide, he would feel responsible and probably be blamed by his superiors.

After his last words, silence lasted for a long time, until

the men gathered outside began to look at one another uneasily. At last Hardy said in a loud and clear voice:

'All right. Get it down.'

Almost at once, there was a click of the key turning in
the lock. The door opened an inch, no more. Hardy moved
towards it as the bigger men stood aside. In view of what
Cellini had said he hardly knew what to expect. A naked
virago, possibly. Some kind of violence? More venomous
tongue-lashing? All the men were obviously agog and
Hardy's heart was beating faster than usual as he pushed
the door wider open.

The woman wasn't there.

He thought: she could be behind the door. The other
door, obviously leading to the bedroom, was wide open:
would she have left it open if she had gone through there?
He pushed this door back firmly but not hard enough to
hurt her if she were hiding behind it, but it went back
against the wall with a bang. He moved fast into the other
room, saw the big four-poster, the love seat, everything
exactly as Cellini had seen it; and he also saw that the window was wide open.

Could she have climbed out?

He put his head out of the window as a man called
sharply, 'That's enough.'

There, outside the ground floor window below, Melinda
Gregory stood with a stick in her hand. She wore a loose-
fitting jumper and long, black pants, and was threatening
a policeman who must have seen her and come hurrying.
As she moved, he put out a hand to restrain her, and two
cameramen broke through the shrubbery, cameras clicking.
The policeman below was distracted by Hardy and looked
up.

'Stop her!' Hardy called.

Melinda Gregory darted to one side, but the man shot
out his right arm and gripped hers. For a few seconds she

struggled furiously, but could not free herself, and other policemen came running until she was surrounded. She was now against the wall, facing the men who blocked her path.

A photographer groaned, 'Oh, hell! I've run out!'

The other photographer was shooting wildly from all angles, and reporters came running. Hardy found himself looking down into the lens of the camera, into the woman's dark hair.

'Hold Mrs. Gregory there,' he ordered. 'I'll be down.'

The others made way for him, and he hurried down the stairs. As he went, he assessed the situation quickly, rue-fully, but faithfully. This woman had put Cellini out of countenance, so that he had hardly known what to do; now she had created a situation which almost baffled him. He was by no means convinced that he had done the right thing; that he hadn't forced the issue simply because Melinda Gregory had been difficult, not because the situation deman-ded it. He still wasn't sure. And he wasn't sure whether he would feel as he did but for the photographers. The front pages of tomorrow's tabloid and 'pop' newspapers were going to be something to see! One woman surrounded by husky men with a Chief Superintendent of Scotland Yard leaning out of the window.

Good God! What would they make of it!

And by far the worst fact was that he had nothing with which to charge the woman. She might possibly be accused of obstructing the police in the course of their duty but a good defending counsel would soon get rid of that! Once he had decided to break the door down he had started a chain reaction which he couldn't stop; his chief hope was that it would soon slacken of its own volition.

Men in the hall were talking.

'What's going on outside?'

'What's going on up there?'

'Johnny's bloody nearly lost his head!'

'Breaking the door down—'

'Tried to kill herself, did she?'

'He wouldn't have had that door down if she hadn't.'

'Hey!' A constable burst in at the front door, face alive with excitement. 'She bloody well jumped the last ten feet from that window. Put up a hell of a fight, too. Fended off old Piggy, Joe and Smithy, one woman and three coppers!'

'What did she do? Kick them in the—'

'Tell you one thing,' interrupted the man who had said 'Johnny's bloody nearly lost his head', 'Johnny's let this one get out of hand.'

'Johnny' appeared at the head of the main staircase, and utter silence fell. He looked as unconcerned as he could, still hurrying, and again men made way for him as he went out of the front door. He felt no particular annoyance or even resentment; everything said had been true, the last the truest of all; he *had* allowed the situation to get out of hand.

No one was in sight when he went outside. He heard voices coming from the left, and turned in that direction. A remarkable scene came into sight when he passed the line of a big bed of geraniums and the ornamental shrubbery. At least ten men, mostly pressmen but with two uniformed and two plainclothes officers, were in a half-circle round Melinda Gregory, who stood with her back against the window looking about her with calm defiance. And Hardy paused in his tracks, because she really did seem magnificent; her attitude more Amazonian than that of any woman he had encountered in a long, long time.

Now was the testing time for him. He could not stand by and do nothing. He could not prevaricate. He must go straight up to the woman and cope. She hadn't seen him yet, but as he drew nearer she turned her head, obviously caught sight of him, and then stared hard. The others, their backs to him at first, turned their heads to see who it was. The tension, already great, seemed to become unbearable. Crossing the line between the men and being nearest to Melinda Gregory was like breaking through an unseen barrier. He became aware of men at the windows, some above his head. It was as if the whole grounds were full of eyes, ready to ridicule him.

And the woman watched him without glancing right or left. She now seemed oblivious of everything and everyone else.

As he drew nearer, he felt the almost mesmeric influence of her eyes; it was as if she were commanding him; seducing him; as if he were walking into a trap from which there could be no escape. He fought this feeling down, and began to smile; and she gave the beginning of a smile, too. Relief surged through him.

Now, they were very near each other, and he did the obvious thing: he put out his hand.

'Hallo, Mrs. Gregory,' he said. 'I'm glad I found you.' Almost mechanically she took his hand. He gripped hers quickly and released it. 'I have to be off in a few minutes but there are one or two questions you can answer, if you will.'

She seemed as taken aback as he had been a few moments before. He put a hand on her arm, and went on, 'Is there a room where we can talk?' Then, aware of men crowding them, he gave a laugh which sounded remarkably natural, and went on, 'It looks as if the Press want a picture. Do you mind being photographed with a policeman?' He moved his position so that they were side by side, and three cameras were levelled at them. He did not take his hand away from Melinda's arm, but after a short moment said crisply, 'That's enough.'

He led her forward. They were almost in front of the Press before reporters began to fire questions at him, and he answered with a brisk directness which was almost brusque.

'Have you any clues, Superintendent?'

'Yes. Dozens.'

'Do you know the thieves?'

'It wouldn't surprise me.'

'Have any of the stolen goods been recovered, sir?'

'Not yet.'

'Is it true that the thieves used a key?'

'No. They forced the front door.'

'Wasn't it locked, barred and bolted, Super?'

'I really can't tell you.'

'How much *was* the loot worth?' a man interrupted.

'In the neighbourhood of three million pounds,' answered Hardy promptly. 'And that really *is* enough.' His hand still lightly resting on Melinda Gregory's arm he led the way back to the house. There was a sudden, seething activity. Like a lot of school children, he thought of his men, but it was affectionately. He had got through and there was no disaster. Now he turned towards the big, denuded room, and opened the door. The woman was looking at him, almost wonderingly. *Watch yourself*, he thought. *Remember Manny*.

'My,' said Melinda, 'what a masterful man you are.'

Then, she went still. She had caught sight of a bare patch on the wall, and after staring at it, began to look about the room, at the blank walls with pale outlines of pictures now gone, empty shelves and recesses, a plain undercarpet where there had been such treasures. And very slowly, she began to cry. She just stood there, the tears rolling slowly down her face.

Superintendent John Hardy wanted only to put his arms about her and to comfort her.

CHAPTER ELEVEN

Whole Truth?

Melinda cried silently, at first. After a few moments her shoulders began to heave, and she seemed to be struggling for breath. She turned round slowly until she had seen every wall and every part of the room, and the expression on her face became more and more piteous. Finally, she looked at Hardy; only at him. Her lips were quivering and the tears rolled faster, to her soft, pink lips, even to her chin.

'What am I going to do?' she asked despairingly. 'What am I going to do?'

Hardy, who felt as if he were divorced from everything but this woman, was oblivious of the men outside, the Press, everyone, as he said hoarsely, 'We'll get everything back.' *What a lunatic thing to say; there was no way of guaranteeing that.*

'But—but you can't,' she mourned.

'Oh yes, we can.' *Don't be a bloody fool.*

'No,' she said. 'I'll never see them again. He's been too clever.'

'Who's been too clever?'

'My—my husband,' answered Melinda Gregory. Now hardness grew in her voice, and she no longer looked piteous, but was almost aggressive. 'He did this.'

'That is a very serious accusation to make,' said Hardy.

She flashed, 'Don't you think I know my own husband? I've lived with him for fifteen years. I know every filthy trick he can pull. I know how he hates me, how he longs to make me suffer. And he's succeeded. At last he's succeeded. If he were standing where you are now, I would kill him.'

It was easy to believe her.

Rage had sent despair into the limbo. Her cheeks were still tear-stained but her eyes were dry and held an unnatural brilliance. Hardy thought: *can she be insane?* Her hands, thrown out in a dramatic gesture, were curled, the painted nails like gaudy claws. Now her breast was rising and falling as if she had difficulty in getting breath.

Then, she cried, 'Get them back!'

The vehemence of the words startled Hardy, who backed a pace.

'We shall do everything we can, and—'

'Get them back! You promised me you would. Get them! It's the only way I can get my revenge on him, it's the only way I can make him suffer. Oh, how I hate that man!'

Hardy felt quite sure that she did; believed that if Gregory were here now she would fly at him. Indeed, she looked as if at the slightest excuse she would fly at him, Hardy. His mood eased: changed. When she had been so despairing he had almost forgotten he was a policeman, had thought only of helping her, but now she was a different person, the woman who had hurled defiance at Carpenter and had locked herself in and tried to run away.

His mind began to work again and possibilities poured in. Could she have hoped to get away? Had she simply put on an act? Was she fooling him, or trying to; had she fooled Cellini? He was sure of one thing: he had never met anyone like her, and it was lucky he hadn't made a bigger fool of himself than he had.

'Mrs. Gregory,' he said. 'I have to ask you some questions —officially.' He strode to the door and opened it, to find Percival just outside, obviously teetering on the edge of coming in. Percival had one great asset: a kind of shorthand which could take down statements at great speed. 'Come in, Inspector,' Hardy said, and to Melinda, 'Mrs. Gregory, this is Detective Inspector Percival.' He was brisk and authoritative again. 'You say you have reason to believe that your husband is responsible for the burglary here. Please sit down.' He himself sat at the desk, and Percival pushed an upright chair forward for Melinda, and sat on another, his notebook open on his knees. 'Are you sure about this?'

'Yes,' she said, harshly.

'You believe your husband to be responsible for the burglary?'

'Yes!'

'Why do you think this?'

'Because he's been threatening to ruin me for years.'

'And how would this burglary ruin you?'

'Everything in this house was mine.'

'Do you mean he made it over to you?'

'I mean I *paid* him for it. He was short of money, he's always short of money, whereas I've plenty. He thinks he's a great financial wizard but he's a witless fool. He needed three million pounds and used the treasures here as security, and *I* got them out of hock in return for them—all the art treasures in this house, and the house itself. It's mine, all mine.'

'Is there a document to establish this as a fact?'

She flashed again, wildly, *'Do you think I'm lying?'*

'If there's no document then in court it could be your word against his.'

'No one would believe the lying beast!'

'Is there a document, Mrs. Gregory?' Hardy found himself losing sympathy with her more every moment.

'Yes,' she answered, sullenly.

'Where is it?'

'You don't think I carry it around with me, do you?'

'I would like to know where it is, Mrs. Gregory.'

'It's at my bank.'

'What is your bank?'

'The Mid-West, in Piccadilly.'

'Thank you. Do I understand you to accuse your husband of planning this burglary (a) because of personal animosity and (b) for gain?'

'Yes, you do,' she said.

'Wouldn't the money from the insurance be paid to you?'

'No,' she answered, roughly. 'I've already told someone this: the insurance was left in his name. And if you think I was weak in the head to leave it that way—then, all right, I was weak in the head! I'm not the business type, he is. And dear God, I let him handle my affairs. I trusted him with my money even if—' She broke off, fingers curling again.

'So your husband will receive the insurance compensation,' Hardy remarked.

'Yes!'

'I doubt it, if this document shows that the stolen goods were yours,' Hardy said. 'Certainly you could get an injunction to have payment deferred until the ownership was established.'

'Goods!' she cried. '*Goods!* A collection of the most wonderful treasures in the world of art, paintings by new masters and by old, sculptures beyond price, antiques which have no equal, *objets d'art* from every corner of the world and from every civilisation, and you call them *goods!* Why, you're a barbarian. You're a savage. You don't deserve to live in a world where people worship beauty and—'

'At the same time worship money,' Hardy broke in brusquely. 'Shall we put an end to these hysterics, Mrs. Gregory, and get on with the job in hand?'

For a moment he thought again that she would fly at him, and Percival actually tossed his notebook aside and started up from his chair. Hardy sat solid and unmoving but his heart thumped wildly as he wondered what she would do.

'You *pig*!' she hissed at him.

'Mrs. Gregory, if you want us to recover the stolen goods, you must co-operate in every way, without wasting time.'

'You promised me—'

'I promised you we would recover them but that pre-supposed your immediate help.'

She dropped back into her chair, pursed her lips sullenly, and then asked in a petulant voice:

'What do you want to know?'

'Have you any evidence that your husband was involved with the burglary?'

'Evidence?' she echoed. 'What do you call evidence? That he arranged for the men to lurk in the grounds every night, to terrify me? That he did everything his twisted mind could think of to drive me away from here? That he was in money trouble again? That he'd lent some tinpot little African country millions and they bilked, like they all do?' She paused for breath but managed to go on before Hardy could speak. 'Evidence! What are the police for if it isn't to get evidence. I tell you he's been robbing me right and left, he's been trying to drive me out of the house, try-ing to drive me *mad*. That's what you want evidence for! He's been trying to drive me mad so that he could have me certified and then he'd have control of all my money.' Her eyes glittered feverishly as she spat the words out. 'Ask the Popples—*they* know. Ask Dr. Selwin—*he* knows. If he doesn't he's as blind as a bat or—'

She broke off, and caught her breath. Percival paused in his notes to look at her and Hardy remembered that she had behaved like this at least twice before, pulling up short in the middle of a torrent of words as if some new and terrible idea had struck her.

She uttered a strangled, 'No.' Then she added in a voice

the others could hardly hear, 'It couldn't *be*!'

When she had been silent for a few seconds Hardy prompted quietly:

'What couldn't be, Mrs. Gregory?'

She stared at him but hardly seemed to know he was there; her expression was one of utter despair; and horror was mixed with it. She did not answer Hardy directly yet the answer was in the whispered words which followed.

'I trusted him absolutely. Jacob couldn't—couldn't be hand-in-glove with Robert. He couldn't do that. He couldn't betray me like that.' She screwed up her eyes as if to fight back tears and went on, 'But if he is, it would explain so much. Why he is always telling me that I must rest, that I'm not strong, that I ought to go away for a long cure. Oh, God! Not Jacob!'

She opened her eyes slowly, but did not appear to notice Hardy as she stared blankly out of the window. Her whole body began to quiver. Hardy waited, and Percival began to fidget with his pencil.

Then: 'Evidence,' she repeated. 'You can get the evidence. I tell you they're driving me mad.'

She stood up, nodding as if in dismissal as she strode out of the room. Percival was just too late to open the door for her. He glanced over his shoulder at Hardy for confirmation, then went after the woman. Hardy made one or two notes to add to Percival's report, which would be typed out. Soon, Percival came back.

'She's gone to her apartment, sir, or suite, or whatever you call it.'

'Are the Popples about?'

'Mrs. Popple was waiting for her, and Popple is in the kitchen.'

'Tell Popple that we shall need to have men in the house throughout the night and he must make arrangements,' Hardy answered. 'And I want Mrs. Gregory followed wherever she goes. In her frame of mind she might do anything.'

Percival didn't speak, but looked his doubts.

'What's on your mind?' demanded Hardy.

'May I speak freely, sir?'

'Yes.'

'I wouldn't trust her an inch,' declared Percival. 'I think she's trying to take everyone for a ride, including that poor devil of a husband. I know I'm prejudiced but I wouldn't like to see *any*one fooled by her. She ought to be on the stage, she's a consummate actress if ever I saw one!'

Hardy said, 'She may well be. Do all I've told you, nevertheless. Then I want to get off to the Yard.'

'Evans will be there when you arrive,' Percival assured him, 'with news from the City.'

*   *   *

Detective Inspector Evans had a long, lean body, a long, lean face with sunken cheeks and high cheekbones, flashing grey eyes and a long, rather mobile nose. His Welsh accent was unmistakable, and in his private life he admitted to being a fervent Welsh nationalist.

'But being in the Police Force, you understand, there isn't a thing I can do about it. No politics, they say. But what is there in life today that isn't tied up in politics? Can you tell me that, now?'

He sat opposite Hardy in Hardy's small office in the new New Scotland Yard, surrounded by glass and by contemporary office furniture. A bright green carpet stretched from wall to wall.

'How did you get on?' Hardy asked.

'Quite well, sir, I think,' replied Evans.

'Is Gregory in any kind of trouble?'

'Not that I could find out, sir, but no one would be surprised if he were.'

'Why?' demanded Hardy.

'Well, Superintendent, he's a rare combination—a banker who takes chances. He's lent a great deal of money to overseas governments at high interest levels, taking mining and mineral rights as security. The countries aren't always solvent, and the rights are sometimes of doubtful value. I'm talking of the new African nations, sir, the emergent nations as some people call them. He's lent money to South American governments, too. Even if one doesn't repay or maintain the interest, he usually gets trading concessions which he can make over to big companies and corporations and so get his money back sooner or later.'

'All straight and above board, then,' said Hardy.

'Indubitably, sir. I've no doubt about that.'

'Are the City people digging for us?'

'As deep as they can, sir, and they will report daily.'

'Thanks,' said Hardy. 'Keep me in close touch.'

He sent Evans off, ran through his own notes and reports which had come in, then telephoned his immediate chief, the Commander of the Criminal Investigation Department, Sir Andrew Wilkinson. Wilkinson was in.

'Yes, come along to my office,' he said.

His office was only a few doors along the passage. It was twice as large as Hardy's and on a corner, so that it seemed all windows, which overlooked more tall modern buildings and a pleasant concourse with bright green lawns below. His carpet was royal blue. He was a large, fat man and he overlapped his chair. His skin was coarse and his jaw massive but he had a small, delicate-looking mouth and very clear, attractive blue eyes.

He listened attentively, and asked no questions, until Hardy said:

'I'd like to show Manny Cellini a transcript of the woman's statement, sir.'

'Yes, I should do that,' Wilkinson approved. 'Have you talked to Dr. Selwin yet?'

'No.'

'What did Gregory himself have to say?'

'He simply seemed shocked, but recovered very well.'

'What's your opinion of the wife's statement?'

'I wouldn't like to voice one yet, sir.'

'H'mm,' said Wilkinson. 'Do you want me to make sure City keeps right on top of this?'

'Yes, please.'

'I will. Have you any idea who did the job?'

'No,' answered Hardy. 'We haven't a clue. There were no prints, no trademarks. We can't trace the tyres—they were new, had no particular blemishes and could be duplicated a thousand times. All we do know from the size is that they were on a large van or truck. Two people as well as one of our Divisional men saw a pantechnicon in the grounds, but no one was really surprised. There is a lot of to-ing and fro-ing from Hethersett. We've collected footcasts from five different pairs of shoes or boots, all rubbersoled and heeled. The raid was very skilfully planned and as skilfully carried out. We've had a general alert out for hours, of course, but no reports of its movements since it was seen at Swiss Cottage early this morning.'

Wilkinson pursed his lips and remarked, 'So we might never get the stuff back.'

'I certainly wouldn't like to put any money on it,' said Hardy.

'Bit gloomy, aren't you?' the senior man observed. 'You don't need telling that the stuff will have to be sold, it won't do the thieves any good in storage. Have you started checking all the possible buyers?'

'Oh, yes,' Hardy answered. 'All the routine's in hand.' He sat back in his chair and went on with great deliberation, 'I have a feeling we won't fully understand this case until we know whether the Gregorys are sane or not.'

'In short, Manny Cellini is the key to it,' his senior officer remarked.

'I think so,' Hardy said, quietly. 'I really think so.'

*   *   *

About that time, Dr. Selwin woke at the Cellinis', said little to Felisa, and left for his home. He had not been there long before a police inspector called on him. He answered the questions, reticent only about the Gregorys. It was as if he were determined to say nothing about them, using his professional integrity as the reason or excuse.

CHAPTER TWELVE

New Quest

Next morning, Dr. Emmanuel Cellini studied the daily newspapers and was pleasantly relieved to find that his photograph was not in a single one. John Hardy, however, figured in each, and in the *Daily Globe* there was a full page picture of the detective looking down from the window at the woman surrounded by a group of men. It was a very telling photograph indeed.

The *Daily Express* went to town on photographs of Melinda Gregory, and Cellini looked across the breakfast table to see his wife poring over them. She glanced up with a beautiful smile which made her appear much younger than her years.

'And this is the woman you sternly rejected?' she asked.

'You see what a saint I am,' said Cellini mildly.

'Or, perhaps, one might say, what a foolish man!'

Cellini's eyebrows shot up, above the top of the *Daily Globe*.

'I am a fool because I am faithful to you?'

'Manny, Manny,' she protested, smiling very tenderly, 'you could lie with a hundred women and still be faithful to me. And you could leave me in peace for the rest of our lives together and yet love only me. You do not need telling that, do you?'

He lowered the newspaper and studied her.

She was the girl he had loved, forty-odd years ago, and

the woman he loved now. There had never been any false
values between them, no half-truths, no pretences. They
had seldom talked of this, but it was so. Each had been
forever the other's and each had been forever his own. Now,
they looked at each other with understanding as well as love,
until Cellini said:

'Do you feel no different?'

'I feel no different,' she confirmed. 'Why should I, my
sweet one?'

'Now that others could perhaps offer more than you,
there is no jealousy in you?'

'After the years we have spent together there could be
no jealousy,' answered Felisa. She leaned across and touched
his hand. 'You are a man. How could you ever be less? Is
your life any the less yours because I share so much of it?
Or mine any the less mine because I share so much?'

'No,' he answered, slowly. 'No, my dear. No.'

'Manny,' she said.

'Yes, Felisa?'

'She is a very beautiful woman.'

'She is very beautiful, yes.'

'And she offered herself to you?'

'She did, Felisa.'

'And you tell me she has all these lovers?'

'Yes, she is said to have lovers by the legion.'

'So one more would make no difference to her.'

'So it would appear.'

'Manny,' asked Felisa, 'is she sick?'

'I think perhaps she is sick.'

'Will you do whatever you must do to help her?' Felisa
asked.

Cellini did not answer.

'Manny,' his wife persisted, 'in what way can you help
her?'

'If there is a way to help, it is to make her tell the truth.'

'Then this you must do,' declared Felisa.

'Do you know what you are saying?' he asked, very gently.

'Yes, my love, I know what I am saying. That despite all her lovers and her husband she still might be a very lonely woman, and she might well confide in a man who made her feel not alone. Manny, I do not need to labour this point, surely. She needs help. You are a man in whose arms she might find the solace and the reassurance that she needs. So: do not deny her. And—' Felisa smiled with a strange gentleness, and she looked not the wife but the mother of this man. 'And do not deny yourself, dear Manny. There is no need.'

He put the newspaper down and raised her hand to his lips and kissed her. For a moment they held each other's gaze, and as they were about to unlock this gaze, the telephone bell rang. The instrument was within Cellini's reach, and he reached for and lifted it quite slowly.

'Dr. Cellini,' he announced. Then in a brighter tone, 'Hallo, John, good morning ... I am rested, thank you ... No, there is no change in my attitude or my thinking ... You *are*?' His voice rose in obvious satisfaction and Felisa put down her newspaper again. 'Good ... Yes, please ... Is there word of Gregory? ... Staying at his club, you say; what a strange affair it is ... And Jacob Selwin ... Yes. Yes, at once, and I will then go and see her this afternoon.' There was a longer pause before he went on, 'John, one thing I believe it would be worth finding out ... The names of her lovers ... A woman who is said to have had so many might well have some rogues among them, rogues who might take advantage of the situation ... It is simply an idea,' went on Manny, and then gave a little splutter of a laugh. '*Indeed!* ... Yes, I am humbled. I should have expected you to be ahead of me ... If I could have a list of them as they are identified, and if you could put alongside each name the age, occupation, social standing and financial standing ... My dear John, of course I will do everything I possibly can. Thank you, I shall expect your message soon.' He put down the receiver and looked across at his wife, obviously jubilant. 'I am to have a copy of the reports of the inquiries at Hethersett yesterday,' he said. 'They will be sent here by special messenger.'

'With reports on both husband and wife?' asked Felisa.

'Yes, to my astonishment. John has concluded that the nature of the people involved will be a most important factor in finding out the truth about the robbery.' He poured himself another cup of coffee, and drank it down. He looked excited as well as gratified, and was oblivious of the humour which his new mood obviously created in his wife.

'Manny,' she said when he got up from the table, 'you look ten years younger. No—*twenty* years.'

'Such flattery,' said Cellini, but he was not ill-pleased. 'Felisa, this morning I will have a chauffeur-driven car. I will read these reports on the way to Robert Gregory's office.'

'It is time you gave up driving,' she said. 'Past time you devoted more time to thinking!'

He was still smiling when, less than half-an-hour later, a woman police officer on a motor-cycle arrived with a sheaf of reports from Hardy. It took only a moment to realise that the reports had been prepared with painstaking thoroughness. He was in the back of a large, old-fashioned car, on the way to the City, when he began to read.

Soon, he was absorbed.

Both Hardy and the man Percival had added comments on the woman's attitude. There were references to her moods, her early surliness, the fact that she had frequently quivered from head to foot. There was a most graphic report of other times when her tone had changed, even what she had looked like when she had threatened to kill her husband. He read on, as his driver coped with heavy traffic at Putney Hill and Putney Bridge, then along New King's Road. As more traffic flowed in from Wandsworth Bridge Road and Harwood Road, through teeming Chelsea and winding Sloane Square, he read and sometimes leaned back and closed his eyes, seeing nothing but the face of the man and the woman.

At Victoria he was reading about the moment when Melinda had climbed out of the window.

At Parliament Square, where tall red buses stood in line and taxis and small cars fussed and fumed, he was at the spot where she had accused her husband.

At Blackfriars he was with her when she was almost in tears, and at the Bank of England she was storming out of the room. That was when Cellini put the reports down and became aware of traffic, the thronged pavements of the narrow streets, the tall grey buildings housing banks and insurance companies and the headquarters of commercial houses which traded all over the world. He was looking at a window box filled with geraniums which reminded him of the beds at Hethersett, when his driver said:

'Number 112, sir.'

'Eh? Oh. Yes. Thank you. Will you drop me here and— oh, dear,' said Cellini, 'where can you wait?'

'I'll find a spot, sir. Supposing I walk back and wait here, then I can get the car when you've finished.'

'Good,' approved Cellini. 'Very good.' He got out, as vast trucks passed and large buses, growling. A man was in a doorway of the next building to the tall and narrow Number 112, and he recognised a man from the City Police. Of course, Gregory's office would be closely watched.

Then, as he reached the dark hall with the old-fashioned open ironwork lift and the stone staircase, he saw Selwin, coming down the stairs. Cellini stood aside, as he would for anyone, but prepared to speak. Instead, Selwin stared straight ahead, and did not see—or at least did not recognise—

Cellini. He was tight-lipped and hard-eyed as he strode past, and his clothes were rumpled.

'Well, well,' murmured Cellini.

A notice board in the hall showed *Gregory & Wolf—3rd Floor*. The lift was humming so he decided to walk up. A man was working on the stonework of the landing on the second floor, and Cellini recognised him as a detective sergeant from the Yard.

'My goodness!' he ejaculated.

At last he reached the third floor, all of which was occupied by *Gregory & Wolf*. A door was marked INQUIRIES, another: *Private*. He went to the private door and tried it, but it was locked. He went into *Inquiries*, and found a pleasant if rather unmodernised office with three girls in it, including one at a small, old-fashioned red switchboard. She looked up, brightly.

'Can I help you, sir?'

'I have an urgent need to see Mr. Gregory. My name is—'

'Oh, I'm ever so sorry, sir, but I don't think Mr. Gregory can see anybody,' the girl interrupted. 'He's cancelled all his appointments for the day, in fact he *may* cancel everything for the rest of the week. I'm ever so sorry, sir.'

'My name is Cellini,' Cellini said. 'Please tell him I'm here.'

'I really don't think he'll see you, sir.'

Cellini, in his mildest voice, pleaded, 'Try, will you, please.'

The girl hesitated, then turned away and plugged in one of her lines. Almost at once she said, 'Kathie, there is a Dr. Cellini who says he has an appointment with Mr. Gregory ... Eh? Oh! Yes, all right then.' She unplugged and gave Cellini a dazzling smile. 'Mr. Gregory's secretary says she'll be right out, sir.'

'Thank you,' murmured Cellini.

'Right out' proved to be about ten minutes. A very small, very mini-skirted girl with slick black hair and too much make-up came out of a door on the right, gave Cellini an aloof smile, and said, 'Mr. Gregory will see you now. Please come this way.'

There was a small office with a desk and a typing desk, a large room where several men worked amid a mass of telephones, and then a heavy, dark brown door marked: R. GREGORY. The girl opened this and stood aside, announcing:

'Dr. Cellini, sir.'

Cellini went in.

This room was pleasant in an old-fashioned way, with a big square desk behind which Gregory sat, two leather armchairs, some filing cabinets and a small table with a dozen telephones on it, all of different colours. Gregory was putting one instrument down as he stood up, and put out his hand.

'Do sit down,' he said, in his most pleasant voice, and motioned to a wooden armchair with a comfortably padded seat. 'I gather from a newspaper chap that you've been having quite a time with my wife, but at least you didn't get your picture in the newspapers. Unlike you, policemen seem to. Your friend Hardy *really* went to town.'

'Or was taken to town,' retorted Cellini.

'Oh. Yes.' Gregory smiled. He seemed absolutely self-assured, all signs of tiredness gone, and was freshly shaven and immaculate. 'It could be.' He contemplated Cellini with a half-amused smile, and then said, 'I've just told Jacob Selwin that I won't want him any more.'

'Have you indeed.' Cellini sat upright in his chair. 'May I ask why?'

'I think he was on my wife's side, and that between them they were persuading me that I was mad. I've decided that I'm not. I've just made a fortune on a deal I thought was going to fall through, and I don't believe madmen can be

clear-headed enough for that.' He gave an amused laugh.
'Do *you* think I'm mad, Dr. Cellini? You're a specialist on
the subject, aren't you?'

Cellini sat up very straight, and answered, 'I don't know
you well enough yet to form an opinion, Mr. Gregory.'

Gregory's mouth dropped open; and then he threw back
his head and roared with laughter, his broad nostrils giving
him an uncanny resemblance to a bull. The laughter went
on long enough to acquire an artificial ring, but at last it
stopped and Gregory said gustily:

'You're a remarkable man! I'm glad I've known you. And
I'm glad that Jacob Selwin's last service was to introduce
us!'

'But you no longer require my professional services,'
Cellini suggested.

'Oh, but I do. I want you to prove the truth: that my
darling Melinda is as mad as a hatter. That woman is going
to kill someone one day, you know. I just told Jacob what I
thought, and asked him to give evidence against her, but he
flatly refused. Do you know what I suspect, Dr. Cellini?'

'What do you suspect, Mr. Gregory?'

'That Jacob and Melinda weren't strictly professional in
their association. Not that I blame Jacob, my wife is the
most practised seducer in the world. One hasn't a chance
when she begins to flaunt her body. It's her body which has
saved her from being certified for a long, long time. Tell
me,' Gregory settled further back in his chair, grinning as
if to prove this didn't hurt, 'do you know her well enough
to judge whether she is certifiable under the Act?'

Very slowly, Cellini shook his head.

'No,' he answered.

'How well do you have to know her before you can form
an opinion?'

'One cannot put a time,' said Cellini. 'Sometimes a day
or two will be enough, sometimes one needs months. What

makes you think she is not sane?'

'Because she keeps threatening to kill me,' Robert Gregory answered.

'That wouldn't necessarily be insanity,' replied Cellini. 'Some very normal people commit murder. They may have illusory motives but one illusion isn't sufficient to prove any person insane. Has she any good and rational reason to wish you dead, Mr. Gregory? Have you in fact been robbing her, and trying to drive her out of her mind?'

CHAPTER THIRTEEN

Man of Good Sense

Manny Cellini knew that his question might deeply offend, might bring on one of Gregory's outbursts of fury, or might bring on a mood of sullen resentment. It was impossible to judge, at first, for Gregory sat absolutely still. Cellini had not really noticed how powerful he was before this.

Then, Gregory relaxed, and gave a fierce grin which wasn't in any way a sign of amusement.

'So she's at that again, is she?'

'She certainly accused you of trying to drive her mad so as to—'

'So as to get my hands on her money,' interrupted Gregory. 'That is so.'

'She's lying. She's lying,' Gregory repeated, heavily.

'She makes her story very convincing,' stated Cellini.

'I don't doubt it. She can be very convincing whatever her mood, especially with men. May I ask whether she has made a pass at you yet?'

'A pass?' echoed Cellini, as if puzzled by the phrase.

Gregory hesitated, then gave a lift of his eyebrows, as if astonished that anyone could be so naïve.

'Never mind. Has she told the police this?'

'Yes.'

'This time it really is war to the finish,' remarked Gregory, his jaw thrusting forward. 'Well, it had to come sooner or later. We've lived a cat and dog life for so long it's difficult to realise that there can be an end to it. I've got a lot of re-thinking to do, and not a lot of time to do it in. She *is* mad, you know. I used to think she was a congenital liar with a bad memory, and a slut, but now I'm sure she is schizo-phrenic. The problem is to prove it, and I can't wait those months you talk about. I just have to know.'

'Why is it so important to you?' asked Cellini, mildly.

'That's a long story, and I'm not sure it's any business of yours.' Gregory sounded near bad-tempered for the first time. 'I want to prove she's mad, that's all. Are you a doctor of psychiatry or aren't you?' When Cellini did not answer at once, he went on roughly, 'Jacob Selwin started behaving like a moralist, that's why I broke with him. Do *you* set yourself up as judge and jury or—'

'Really!' exclaimed Cellini. 'I think you must be one of the silliest men I've ever talked to. *Really!* When one dis-cusses such an issue with a person of education and intellig-ence one does expect at least the rudiments of common sense.' He placed his hands on the arm of his chair and stood up, abruptly. 'I have wasted far too much time on this affair already. There are too many people who really need help and understanding, not simply indulgence, for me to waste time here. Good morning.'

Gregory sat back, hands gripping the arm of his chair, amazed. Cellini, nearly as angry as he sounded, was sure of one thing: unless he could get the co-operation he wanted this case *was* a waste of time. And heart-case or not, Gregory needed strong handling. He espied a chair leg which jutted out and avoided it; the last thing he wanted was to fall on his face.

'Cellini!' called Gregory.

'I really will *not* go on like this.'

'Cellini, what the hell are you talking about?' There was a rumble of movement, of Gregory pushing his chair back, and when Cellini glanced over his shoulder the man was standing up, massive as an ox.

'You mean you don't *know*?' breathed Cellini.

'Of course I don't know. What made you go off the deep-end like that?'

Cellini turned round, shaking his head as if in disbelief. There was quiet in the office, broken by the sound of traffic from the street. A shaft of sunlight struck the side of Gregory's head and in that moment he was impressively strong-looking. A telephone bell rang outside, and a moment later, a bell rang on Gregory's battery of instruments and a light showed on one of them. He snatched it up.

'I'll call back.' He didn't wait for any response but banged the receiver down. 'Well? Were you just being rude for the sake of it?'

'Mr. Gregory,' said Cellini, 'madness in all its forms is a difficult state to diagnose and to identify. There is a little madness in all of us, but most of us manage to conceal it well, and are often unaware of it. And while it may be congenital, or the result of a fall or accident, it can also be the result of environment, of pressures which weigh upon a mind already weakened, until it breaks. I can tell you this. By many standards, your wife is quite sane. But she shows certain indications of instability and it is conceivable that this does, at times, make her not responsible for her actions. This might be insanity within the legal meaning of the term. However, even people adjudged insane are subject to certain provisions and restrictions. One may be insane, for instance, but not violent or in any way dangerous; there would be no legal compulsion to have such a person kept under control. Such persons may often be completely res-ponsible in many ways, however. I have known a person detained in a private asylum whose knowledge of the stock market and whose dexterity in handling shares is such that he makes millions of pounds for his estate. Madness or in-sanity, after all, is little more than an extension of eccentricity, and eccentricity is an extension of normality. There are people with positive genius for making money, or for organisation, or other specific abilities, who are dull and useless in almost any other form of activity.'

Gregory, sitting down with his hands on the arms of his chair, was listening intently.

'There is another kind of insanity within the meaning of the Act which is well-known and yet often extremely difficult to identify,' went on Cellini. 'Often the madness only reveals itself under the stimulus of external incidents. One common form is persecution complex. There are a surprising number of people who are perfectly happy and normal indoors, or in company, but who are convinced they are being followed whenever they are out of doors on their own. Some are all right on bright days; others—most commonly known but by no means the most common in occurrence—are afflicted at certain phases of the moon. Some are affected by colours, others by odours, others by people, others by animals, others again by plants. The task in each case is to find the symptoms or the signs of madness, and then discover the cause. It is quite impossible to discover the cause within a reasonable time, unless one is fully aware of the background, the likely causes, the conditions which may influence certain attitudes of mind.'

For the first time since launching this diatribe, he paused: but Gregory sat and watched, as if fascinated.

'Now I trust you will understand why it is essential for me to know the full circumstances—about you, your wife, what makes you so angry at times, what makes her at times most reasonable and gentle and at other times angry and turbulent,' Cellini went on. 'Insanity may be a condition of the mind, and so of the brain, but it is nearly always sparked, as it were, by these different factors. So, if I am to be at all helpful, I need to know why you are so influenced, why it is important to you that your wife be certified insane, and what are the factors which create her different moods, her spasms, as you would have me believe, of insanity.'

Now, he finished; and he went back to his chair. He was perspiring gently, but he did not dab at his forehead or his neck, just waited for Gregory's reaction.

Gregory said in a very flat, considered voice, 'She is very wealthy in her own right, while she and I are joint trustees of a substantial fund, a family legacy which on our deaths will go to charitable foundations. I want to use the funds for certain major investments which would yield great dividends. She refuses to take chances. Her objections are absurd. I think they're because she's convinced I want to rob and cheat both her and the trust. She sometimes thinks I want to force her to divorce me, but if we were divorced I would lose my say in this fund. I need to stay married to her. I've come to hate the sight of her. I don't propose to live under the same roof again, but I shall not divorce her, whatever provocation she gives me, nor no matter how often—' He broke off and coloured deeply, then waved his hands as if waiving the subject.

'No matter how many lovers she takes,' murmered Cellini.

'I've no wish to discuss that,' barked Gregory.

Cellini looked at him steadily and in silence for some time, and then shifted slightly in his chair. He felt what he had not felt for this man until now; compassion.

'Mr. Gregory,' he said. 'You have been living under a great strain, I imagine for a long time. I don't know all the causes. I do know that your reaction to your wife's behaviour or attitudes could influence her behaviour. I have reason to believe that you have been terribly distressed by your wife's habit of taking lovers—'

'I'm bloody *damned* if I'll let you talk like that!' Gregory roared.

'Mr. Gregory,' said Cellini, 'more distress comes from a human being's compulsion to keep unpalatable facts to himself than you will ever realise. I *am* a doctor. I *am* a psychiatrist. I will solemnly promise that I will discuss this particular subject with no one else, except possibly your wife. And as a doctor I assure you that if you bottle up these things much longer they will burst out of you with such explosive force that you could do great harm, to yourself and to others. I think your heart spasms may be due to these emotional pressures not to physical weakness. You will have to see this in order to cure yourself.'

Gregory was champing as if at a bit. His face was ashen grey and his eyes glittering and narrowed. For a while it seemed as if he intended to say nothing, but at last he ground out:

'If you mean I might kill my wife, say so.'

'I mean you might kill your wife, injure anyone who tried to stop you, and end up either by killing yourself or spending the most productive years of your life in prison. Mr. Gregory, I beg you talk freely to me.'

After another long silence, Gregory muttered, 'Oh, what the hell! What do you want to know?'

'First let me tell you what I want you to do,' said Cellini, quietly. 'I want you to answer my questions freely and if possibly objectively and at all costs truthfully. If you feel that you must thump the table, then thump the table. If you feel you must roar at the top of your voice, then roar.'

'What if I want to break your neck?' growled Gregory.

'Then, obviously, you must try.' Cellini smiled. His body was so diminutive against the other that laughter was the only resort. And both of them laughed, Gregory on a hard, tense note.

'Go on,' he ordered.

'Thank you. Do you love your wife, Mr. Gregory?'

Gregory clenched his fist.

'Love that whore— My God I don't!'

'I think you do,' stated Cellini quietly.

'You sit there and have the bloody impudence to tell *me* that you know more about my emotions than I do! I'll tell you something,' went on Gregory, 'you're a bloody quack.'

'I have been told that before,' Cellini retorted.

'It's still true.'

'I think you are deeply in love with your wife, Mr. Gregory.'

'Then you're a bigger bloody fool!'

'Do you resent it when your wife takes a lover?'

'My God, I'll break your neck!' roared Gregory springing to his feet. 'Get out of this office. Never come back!' But he did not round his desk, just stood glaring at Cellini, who did not get up, did not look away, and scarcely blinked.

'Mr. Gregory,' he asked in a soft voice, 'does it hurt as much now as when you first began to suspect?'

Gregory stood so stiff and tall that it was almost as if he had been turned to stone. There was even a bleakness about his eyes, which lost their glitter and became glazed. At last, very slowly, he began to lower himself into his chair, and when he was sitting down he seemed to groan three words, which were quite unmistakable.

'It is worse.' There was another pause, then another groan, 'A lot worse. Sometimes, I—' He broke off, and closed his eyes, and sat there unmoving, until at last Cellini murmured:

'Thank you, Robert. Thank you very much. Do you think anyone else is aware of this?'

'Jacob Selwin knows.' Gregory did not open his eyes or raise his voice. 'He's known for a long time. I always thought he was on my side, but if he's on Melinda's—'

Gregory broke off.

'You know, you really aren't seeing this very straight,' remarked Cellini. 'Selwin is your family doctor. He must be able to see much more of the truth than either of you. He must be as familiar with your side, as you call it, as he is with your wife's. In an effort to keep you together, in fact to bring you back together, he must have had an extraordinarily difficult time. You were adamant, for many months, about your refusal to see me. You demanded too much of him.'

'He's been my doctor all my life,' Gregory muttered. 'He owed me his loyalty.'

'He owes all his patients the best attention he can give them,' Cellini chided, gently. 'Now that he will not try to prove one patient insane in order to serve another's purpose, you lose your temper and throw him out.'

'How the devil do you know I threw him out?' demanded Gregory.

'His collar was rucked up and his tie pulled to one side and his hair dishevelled,' answered Cellini. 'Well, sir. You want your wife to be certified insane so that you can invest certain moneys now in trust and of which you are both the trustees. If one or the other were to die or be incapacitated, then the remaining one would be the only trustee. Is that right?'

'Yes.'

'Why won't your wife accept your advice on the investments?'

'Because she's too timid and won't take the slightest risk.'

'*Should* trustees take risks?' inquired Cellini.

'This kind of risk, yes. I'm a successful commercial banker and *I* take risks.'

'That is part of your business, but you don't take too many risks or you wouldn't be able to boast that you're successful.' remarked Cellini. 'What did you do with the three million pounds your wife paid you for the treasures at your home?'

This time, the effect was almost as if he had dropped a bomb. Gregory actually rose in his chair and then dropped back into it, as if he were utterly devastated. Then, slowly, he began to turn colour and the blueish tinge which betrayed cardiac trouble began to suffuse his cheeks and his lips. Deliberately but slowly, Cellini leaned forward, and felt for the little bottle in the pocket of Gregory's coat. He found it, shook a tablet out and held it between his thumb and forefinger close to Gregory's lips. He picked up the carafe of water and poured out with his free hand, then held the glass up.

'Take this, Mr. Gregory.'

Gregory just sat there.

'*Take this!*' rapped Cellini, and he pushed the tablet between the other's lips, then placed the glass against his lips. 'And drink this—at once!'

As if in a trance, Gregory obeyed. Cellini sat back, contemplating and reflecting. He had risked bringing on this attack but there was no danger from it, since the tablet would act so quickly. And it was possible that Gregory could induce such attacks. Melinda always put on an act when there was something she didn't want to discuss, and possibly whenever she wanted to deceive him. Gregory's could be the same kind of conscious or subconscious reaction. It could also be a kind of subconscious defence mechanism, something which developed whenever Gregory was thrown off his guard. The only way to be sure of either was to have him examined during or immediately after one of these spasms, and arranging for an examination might be next door to impossible.

Slowly, Gregory recovered, but something seemed to have happened to him. His breathing was shallow, and his body limp; it was almost as if he had suddenly lost all hope. Cellini had a feeling that it would be useless to try to force any more questions now. He was reluctant to give up, but it would be folly to push a truly unwilling patient.

Then, Gregory said huskily, 'Now I *know* she's mad. She didn't pay me anything, and I've never borrowed anything from her. Did she say she had a document to prove this?'

'She did indeed,' said Cellini.

'I think that's how she fooled Jacob,' Gregory muttered. 'That must have been it. Well, here's something your friends the police can prove, Cellini. Have them find the document. Just let them try. They can't find it because it doesn't exist. She is too mean and too timid to make money available to me.' His voice rose. '*Love* her? At times I hate her. She—'

A telephone bell rang and a light glowed; he did exactly as he had before, and banged the receiver down. Then he glared as if challenging Cellini to defy him. Before either man spoke, the door opened, and the big-eyed, mini-skirted girl came in.

'Your man Popple is calling, sir,' she said, perfectly calmly. 'He says it's very urgent. Will you take the call?'

Gregory seemed to pale, but he answered without hesitating, 'Yes.' He flicked on a switch at the little box as the girl disappeared. A moment later the girl spoke very clearly, but behind the voice was the sound of laboured breathing.

'Mr. Gregory is on the line, Mr. Popple.'

'Mr. Gregory!' gasped Popple, pausing between words. 'Miss Melinda is having a terrible quarrel with Dr. Selwin. Please come. Please come at once!'

CHAPTER FOURTEEN

The Quarrel

'You've got to leave him,' Selwin rasped.

'You're as mad as he is,' hissed Melinda; and it sounded as if she really meant to hiss.

'I tell you he's driving you mad.'

'I tell you *I* know what I'm doing.'

'You don't—you never have. You should never have married—'

'Don't tell *me* what I should have done fifteen years ago!'

'If I'd known you better then—'

'I suppose you'd have married me yourself. Smooth young doctor weds society heiress. Wouldn't the headlines have rejoiced you.'

'You've got to leave him,' Selwin repeated, harshly. 'You don't love him. My God, you've had a hundred lovers, and every one's an insult to him. Why the devil you don't leave him—'

'Perhaps I like insulting dear darling Robert.'

'You're hurting yourself more than you're hurting him.'

'For a doctor you would make a *very* good laboratory assistant.'

'Melinda, don't you understand that you're killing yourself?'

'I thought you said he was driving me mad.'

'It comes to the same thing.'

'Get out of here!' Melinda suddenly screamed at him.

'*I don't ever want to see you again. Get out!*'

'Melinda—'

'*Just get out!*' she screeched.

He did not move an inch. His face was set and only two spots of colour showed on his cheeks. He looked ill to the point of exhaustion. His lips were parted slightly to show his fine teeth; it was curiously like a snarl.

'*Get out!*' she cried again, and struck him savagely across the face.

He reeled to one side, and she pushed at him as if suddenly intent on thrusting towards the door. He did not make any attempt to save himself, but slipped and fell. She stood over him, kicking at him—his stomach, his ribs, his knees, his legs—and then suddenly at his groin. He pushed her foot away instinctively, and she staggered in turn, recovered her balance and drove her pointed shoe towards his middle. Again he pushed her foot away. Now, he was on his side, knees drawn up defensively. He could see the pale fury of her face and the glitter in her eyes, the rage—perhaps the madness.

She kicked again.

This time, he grabbed and held her ankle and she was helpless on one leg. Hopping, and supporting herself with a hand against the wall, she screamed:

'Let me go! Let me go!'

*   *   *

Outside, in the passage, the Popples stood in new alarm, until Maxine gripped her husband's arm and whispered, 'You must telephone Mr. Robert. *Hurry*. Before the police find out what's going on. *Hurry*.'

And Popple turned and hurried along to his room, leaving his wife outside the door, straining her ears to catch what was being said. She could not catch all the words, now; they seemed to be growling at each other, like wild animals.

*　　*　　*

'Let me go!'

'Don't kick me again,' Selwin growled, and he released her ankle. 'Understand.'

Even before she fully recovered her balance, she kicked at him again and the toe of her shoe caught his knee cap, causing sharp pain. He gasped, screwed himself up almost into a ball, and felt her kick again and again. She had gone absolutely berserk, obviously had no self-control at all, she wanted to hurt, hurt, hurt. She kept muttering in savage undertones and he couldn't distinguish the words, until two began to separate themselves from the others.

' ... *kill you* ... *kill you* ... *kill you* ... '

He was breathing much more evenly, had won the respite that he needed. She drew back her leg to kick again, but he rolled over, away from her, and because her foot met no resistance, she staggered and almost fell. He bounded to his feet and grabbed her.

'Stop it, Melinda!'

She bared her teeth and tried to butt his nose with her head. He slapped her, making a sharp crack of sound, but instead of quietening her it made her more wild and she flung herself at him and beat him about the head and face and tried to bring her knees up into him. He was carried back by the fury of the onslaught, and banged against the wall, but it did not hurt him. Suddenly, he gripped both her wrists with one hand, and put his free arm round her shoulders, holding her very tightly. He could feel the heat of her body. She struggled on as if not a single muscle would keep still. He gradually forced her to stillness, and freed her hands, but before she could press them against his chest he put his other arm round her, so that she could hardly move.

'Stop it.'

'I'll kill you.'

'Stop fighting, Melinda!'

'I'll *kill* you!'

'If you don't stop you'll go crazy!'

'*I'll kill you.*'

'Melinda—you need a shot.'

'You've given me your last shot. Let me go!'

She was struggling furiously, and speaking in a growling undertone. Suddenly she butted him in the nose, sent anguish through him and made stinging tears rush to his eyes. She made a great effort to free herself, but he held on. Now she kicked at his shins, but had little room in which to manoeuvre.

Suddenly, he shifted his hold, and lifted her. One moment she was writhing and struggling, hugged tightly to him, the next he held her over his shoulder, hoisting her high. Startled, at first she did not kick. He carried her out of the dressing-room and into her bedroom. As she began to thrash the air with her legs, he flung her on to the big, white bed, and before she could get up, straddled her with his arms. Now, she was practically helpless.

'Lie still,' he ordered. 'You'll hurt yourself if you don't.'

She lay still.

Gasping for breath, her mouth wide open, her eyes almost closed, it was as if she were at last in a state of exhaustion. Her whole body relaxed. Very slowly, he took the weight of his body away from her, and she did not fling herself in a wild paroxysm again. Soon, he was able to sit on the side of the bed, not restraining her. She showed no sign that she was aware of him. He took a slim case out of his pocket, and opened it. A small hypodermic syringe and several ampoules were fitted into the case. Still breathing hard, he took out one of the ampoules and then the syringe, and plunged the needle in, gradually draining the liquid. The syringe was ready at last and he turned to her.

She was staring at him, round-eyed.

'Don't worry, Melinda,' he said. 'You'll be all right.'

'What—what's that?'

'Just a sedative, you'll be all right.'

'I *am* all right!'

'Yes, you're much better. Hold out your left arm.'

She looked at the hypodermic syringe, then at him, moved her left arm slowly, and began to push up the half-length sleeve. Then, without any warning, she struck his hand aside, and the needle and case went flying across the room. He sprang up, catching his breath.

'I don't want any more sedatives!' Her voice was hideously strident.

'Melinda, you need rest.'

'I've had too much rest.'

'You don't understand,' Selwin said in an almost pleading voice. 'You need rest. You can't go on like this. Living cat and dog with Robert is driving you crazy. I'm serious, Melinda. You need to sleep now, and then you need to think seriously about going away without him.'

Her eyes were narrowed and her breathing much less laboured. She spoke with quiet deliberation.

'My living with Robert is driving *you* crazy, you mean.'

'Melinda—'

'You'd give your right arm to come away with me, wouldn't you?'

'Melinda, I am your doctor.'

'Jacob,' she said, in a sneery voice, 'what happens after you put me to sleep?'

'Happens? You wake up feeling much better, of course.'

'I don't mean what happens when I wake up, but just after I've gone off.'

'You rest, that's all.'

'You're a liar,' she accused.

He went very, very pale.

'Don't talk like that, Melinda.'

'I'll talk any way I like,' she said. 'When did you start?'

'I don't know what you're talking about.'

'You know as well as I do,' she said. 'Answer me. When did it start?'

'I tell you I don't know—'

'*When did you start raping me?*' demanded Melinda.

'Melinda!'

'Well—when did you?'

'It—it's a preposterous thing to say.'

'The truth often *is* preposterous. *When did you start?*'

'Melinda, you're not well.'

'I'm perfectly well,' she said. 'Tell me—when did you first get the idea of putting me to sleep and then lying with me, and then hinting that I was going mad—so that if I remembered anything that happened you would be able to dismiss it as a delusion?'

Selwin was sweating freely. His pallor made his eyes seem unnaturally bright. His hands and his arms were aquiver, and his lips were unsteady, too.

'There's not a word of truth in it,' he muttered.

'*I* say it's the truth.'

'Melinda, even a whisper that such a thing happened could ruin me.'

'Should *I* worry if you are ruined? *When did you start, Jacob?*'

He drew away from the bed, and standing up he seemed much more composed and had a dignity which, squatting on the bed, he had not shown. His voice was calmer, too.

'It's no use trying to frighten me,' he said.

'Frighten? I will ruin you if you don't tell the truth.'

'I have never raped you,' he stated.

'That's a lie!'

'It is the simple truth.'

'It is a lie. Just imagine what it would look like in the newspapers,' she said. '*The News of the World*, for instance.'

'It would be the wickedest libel,' he said, dry-tongued.

'It would drive you out of the country,' said Melinda, viciously.

'Yes, it might,' he conceded.

'When did you first take advantage of me, Jacob? Was it after I'd lost my temper one day and sprawled back here with my skirt rucked up? Was it too much for you, good, prudish Jacob?' She looked down at her beautiful legs, covered only just below her torso; seductive beyond words. 'Was it *so* easy and tempting, Jacob? So easy to slip down my—'

'Stop it, Melinda!'

'Jacob,' she said, leaning on one elbow and looking at him from narrowed eyes, 'Robert is mad.'

He didn't answer.

'Robert is mad and I want that proved.'

He still didn't answer.

'If you don't find *some* way of proving it, with or without the help of funny little Manny Cellini, I shall tell the police that you have made a practice of putting me under sedation and then raping me.'

He shook his head, very slowly and deliberately.

'I shall deny it completely, and you could not possibly prove it.'

'Couldn't I?' asked Melinda, in a soft, cruel voice.

'It is impossible to prove it.'

'A witness could prove it, Jacob dear.'

'No witness could prove what is not true,' Selwin said, but he closed his eyes as if assailed by a sudden weight of fear. 'I have never—'

'Mrs. Popple would give evidence,' Melinda declared. 'She first told me you behaved oddly here, and I told her to keep quiet. That was months ago.'

He opened his eyes slowly, and they were filled with pain. 'She was lying. I don't believe she would lie in court.'

'Don't you?' asked Melinda. 'Even if it were a lie, and it wouldn't be, don't you think she would perjure herself for me, Jacob? *I* think she would. She and Popple are the only two people I can trust. I used to think I could trust you, even after learning what you were doing I trusted you, but I don't trust you, now. I wanted you to consult Emmanuel Cellini so as to prove Robert was insane, but he's on Robert's side. *You* are, too, and—'

'Melinda,' Selwin interrupted, 'Robert thinks I am favouring you. He told me that he wouldn't want my services as a doctor any longer. I came here to tell you that.' He broke off, staring as if hopefully, and there was something pathetic in his manner.

She actually laughed.

'It's not your day, Jacob,' she remarked, almost gaily. 'You really don't want to lose *me*, too, do you? I want you to find a way of proving that Robert is as crazy as a coot, and if you don't—'

'No,' he interrupted. 'I shall do nothing more. I've kept trying to keep the peace with both of you but that's all over. You'll either have to be guided by Cellini or get someone else. In these last few minutes, I've decided that it's madness to go on. You know why I have put up with so much, Melinda, don't you?'

'You've made a fortune out of me,' she replied sharply.

'No,' he answered. 'No, that's not it. *Is* it possible that you don't know?' A wondering note sounded in his voice and he frowned, as if at something incredible.

'You've made a fortune,' she stated again.

'I could take as much money out of any one of a dozen patients who wouldn't give me a tenth of the trouble I get from you,' he stated. 'No, there's a very different reason. Melinda, I *did* think you knew.'

'Knew what?' she demanded, almost angrily.

'That I love you,' declared Jacob very simply. 'I love you. I thought you knew. I have put you above everything. Sometimes I think I could put you above life itself.'

CHAPTER FIFTEEN

Witness

There was a long, long silence. Selwin did not move and
Melinda eased away from him, as if she were both startled
and touched. Then, slowly, she began to smile, and slowly
the smile grew into a chuckle and the chuckle into a laugh.
She threw her head back and thrust her bosom forward,
and her laughter grew louder until it seemed almost as if
she had lost all self-control.

Selwin sat there, white to the lips; he hardly seemed to
be breathing.

At last, Melinda stopped, and wiped her eyes with the
tips of her fingers, then threw up her hands in a helpless
gesture.

'So *that's* your excuse,' she mocked.

In a husky voice, Selwin echoed, 'Excuse?'

'For your little sex games with me.'

'There is no truth in that at all,' Selwin stated, coldly.

'You forget my witness.'

'I don't believe—' began Selwin, and then he broke off,
for there was a tap at the door.

It came without warning, and sounded very sharp, even
peremptory. Melinda glanced from him towards the door,
which was still open. It was almost incredible that he should
have heard no one approach.

Then Melinda called, 'What is it, Maxine?'

'Excuse me, Miss Melinda,' said Maxine Popple, 'but

Mr. Robert and Dr. Cellini have just arrived.'

'Where is Popple?' asked Melinda.

'At the head of the stairs, Miss.'

'Have him tell them I will be down in a few minutes,' ordered Melinda, 'and then come back here.'

'Very good,' Maxine answered.

Presumably, she turned away, but she made no sound at all, until after a moment the outer door creaked. Selwin, now on his feet, looked round at the door as Melinda asked in a silky tone:

'You didn't know she had a key, did you?'

He didn't answer.

'Or that she can move as stealthily as a cat,' went on Melinda. 'It was one day when she couldn't understand why you were still here that she came in and saw you, Jacob. You really don't have any choice, you know. You have to do what I tell you.'

He didn't speak, just stood looking down at her, until there was a faint rustle of sound and Maxine Popple's voice sounded from the other side of the door.

'Did you want me, Miss Melinda?'

'Yes. Come in,' Melinda ordered, and the woman came in with that uncanny silence.

In her way she was quite attractive, and certainly not so old as Popple. She did not appear to be in any way disconcerted at the sight of Selwin, who moved so that he could see both the woman on the bed and the woman at the door. His lips were set tightly and he was breathing heavily.

'Maxine,' said Melinda, 'isn't it true that on at least one occasion you saw Dr. Selwin in this bedroom, with me, when I was unconscious and helpless? And didn't you see Dr. Selwin on the bed with me?'

In the silence which followed Selwin caught his breath, to stop from crying out. He looked hard at the woman and she returned his imploring gaze quite calmly.

'Yes, Miss Melinda,' she stated simply.

'Thank you,' Melinda Gregory said. 'That's all for now, Maxine. We may want to hear the story again, later.'

Maxine turned and went out.

Melinda gave Selwin a half-smile, and then asked sweetly, 'You didn't realise there would be a witness, did you, Jacob dear? But you really needn't worry. Maxine is intensely loyal to me and she won't breathe a word, not even to her husband, unless I tell her to. And I don't *want* the scandal to break, I assure you. You would be the villain of the piece, but imagine what a golden tit-bit of gossip there would be every time I appeared in public.' She paused, stretched out her hand, and appeared to want him to take it. 'Let's be sensible, Jacob. Let's work together against Robert, then there will be no scandal, nothing to worry about, I promise you.'

He stared at her for a long time, as if in disbelief: then he spun on his heel and went out of the room.

'Jacob!' she called. 'Come back, or I'll tell them!'

He did not answer, and he did not return.

*   *   *

Dr. Cellini sat by Robert Gregory's side in his, Cellini's, hired car, glad that Gregory had not been at the wheel. He had been desperately upset by Popple's message, and kept twisting and turning in his corner, lighting cigarette after cigarette and then tossing each out of the window. Whenever a bus or lorry obstructed them he swore viciously, and twice bellowed at the driver:

'Why can't you get a move on?'

The driver, to Cellini's gratification, took no notice of this. But he knew the district well, got through until he reached Euston Road, and took short cuts until he was nearly at Hampstead almost before Cellini realised it, and Cellini felt that he could safely talk to him. He arranged for the man to go back to his garage and to send a self-drive hire car here, which would now suit his purpose best. Hardly was that settled than they turned into the driveway of Hethersett. A uniformed policeman was in sight, along the carriageway, and the front door was ajar. One man in plainclothes was in the hall, but otherwise the house had a bare and empty look, and their footsteps resounded on bare boards. Robert Gregory led the way, striding far ahead of Cellini, who felt anxious, not sure that the other man would not plunge into violence.

Jacob Selwin appeared at the head of the main flight of stairs.

He looked far more dishevelled than he had been at the office, and his pallor and his tension were greater too. He did not start or stand back when he saw the two men, but stood on the landing, waiting.

'What the hell have you being doing to Melinda?' demanded Gregory in a voice which seemed to shake the few pictures left on the wall. He bounded up the stairs two at a time. 'Come on. Out with it!'

Selwin said huskily, 'The question is what Melinda has done to me.'

'Don't hedge! Where is she? What have you done to her?'

'She is in her room,' answered Selwin. 'She has just accused me of raping her after I had placed her under sedation. It is, of course, a lie.'

He stopped.

Gregory, only a few stairs in front of him, and still having to look up, stopped also. It was as if he had been shocked beyond words. Selwin swallowed hard, then went on, 'I don't think it is a case of hallucinations. I think she has invented the story and also prevailed on the woman Popple to support it, out of hatred both for you and for me.' He paused long enough to allow Gregory to speak, but all Gregory did was to breathe heavily through his nose; grampus-like. 'I will be at my home for the rest of the day,'

Selwin went on. 'If I should be called out on an emergency, my wife will know where I am.'

He moved to one side, and started down the steps, but before he drew level with Gregory, Gregory shot out an arm to stop him.

'You stay here until I get to the truth of this,' he roared.

Jacob Selwin gave him one long, searing look, and then moved to pass. Gregory rushed at him, but Selwin brushed him aside, continuing his way down the stairs without giving the other man a glance. His expression as he approached Cellini seemed to imply, 'Don't try to stop me.' Cellini moved to one side, watching the man who had first brought him here. He had never seen anyone in greater emotional distress, never seen more anguish in a man's eyes. He did not speak or make any attempt to stop him, but turned and watched as he reached the hall.

Cellini began to follow Selwin, who was at the open front door, when there was a sharp exclamation from the stairs.

'Robert!' cried Melinda, and she added in a tone of alarm, '*Robert!*' She began to run towards her husband, as the plainclothes man who had been checking some measurements came from the big room.

'What—' he began.

'Have Dr. Selwin followed,' Cellini said urgently. 'Confirm with Mr. Hardy when you can but don't let Dr. Selwin out of your sight.' He was half-prepared for some kind of obstructiveness from the other, a sharp-featured man whom he had seen before, but the detective said briskly, 'Right, sir,' and moved off. Over his shoulder, he called, 'Look after Mr. Gregory, won't you?'

'I will indeed,' Cellini assured him, and turned round.

Melinda was kneeling on the stairs, and Robert Gregory's head was on her lap. His legs were at an odd angle, one pointing upwards the other flopping down the stairs. There seemed no sign of a heart spasm. Melinda was patting his

cheeks, quickly but softly, and as Cellini appeared she turned
to him as if in alarm.

'Get the Popples,' ordered Cellini.

'But—'

'Get them!' Cellini repeated peremptorily. 'I'll look after
your husband.'

She rested Gregory's head on a stair and stood up, with
flowing grace, then hurried away. Cellini felt the downward
flopping leg, made sure there were no bones broken,
straightened it, then stepped over Gregory and felt the other
leg, then straightened that. There was ample room to allow
Gregory to stretch across the stairs but not enough for him
to lie there without falling further, so Cellini knelt on the
stair below, taking his weight, and looked into his face. His
lips were moving slightly, his breathing seemed to be normal.
With great care, Cellini felt his head, and touched what
seemed to be a new, rather soft bump at the base of the
skull. Next, he checked ribs and arms and found nothing
to suggest a fracture. By the time he had finished, Popple
and Melinda had appeared. He gave them no chance to
speak, but ordered:

'Popple, take Mr. Gregory's shoulders. I'll take his legs.
Mrs. Gregory, please go ahead and get a bed ready. Popple.'
He had never sounded more sharp or authoritative. 'You
lead the way, walking backwards.'

They hoisted Gregory and began to carry him, Melinda
meekly going on before. Slowly they eased him up the
second stage of the staircase, opposite to Melinda's rooms.
Melinda disappeared into a room on the left, and when
Cellini went in, holding the unconscious man's legs, he saw
that this was a dressing-room and that a bedroom led off,
exactly as Melinda's. Her shadow, moving, was on the door
of the next room, and when they went in, the sheets of a
double bed had been turned down, and Melinda was spread-
ing a towel at the foot, obviously so that Gregory's shoes

should not touch the bedclothes.

Popple lowered Gregory's head to the pillows, breathing very heavily.

'Take it easy for a few minutes,' Cellini ordered, then said to Melinda, 'Have you a doctor other than Dr. Selwin?'

'I—' she began, and then abruptly, 'No.'

'Then telephone Dr. Norris, at Heath Lodge, Hampstead, and ask if he can come at once. Mention my name, please.' Then reassuringly, 'I do not think there is anything seriously wrong, but we'd better be sure.'

She hesitated, looked at Gregory again, and then crossed to a telephone on the other side of the room. Popple, hovering, was getting his breath back slowly. Melinda began to speak on the telephone, and at that moment Gregory turned his head slightly. And almost at the same moment Mrs. Popple entered the room, took one glance at Gregory and cried:

'Oh, my goodness!'

'Some coffee, at once, please,' ordered Cellini. Then he added as if to himself, 'Sooner or later we shall get the truth out of this household.'

Maxine Popple missed a step, but did not look round. Melinda finished on the telephone and turned to say, 'He'll be here in five minutes.' Cellini motioned Popple out of the room, and he went without protest, leaving Cellini alone with Melinda except for the unconscious Gregory. Cellini turned with great deliberation and looked at the woman. He remembered the scene only the previous afternoon, how he had felt, how he had nearly behaved. Melinda was looking at him with a curious kind of defiance.

'Mrs. Gregory,' he said, 'if Dr. Selwin should kill himself the responsibility will be entirely yours.'

She looked astounded.

'What on earth—'

'The time has come when you must realise that you cannot

continue to behave in the way you are doing,' Cellini interrupted. 'You falsely accused Dr. Selwin of a particularly deplorable crime. You appear to have suborned a witness who will be believed. I don't know why you have chosen to disgrace Dr. Selwin but he is an old friend of mine, and I for one will do everything to protect him and if necessary protect his memory.'

'You talk as if he's going to kill himself!'

'And so he might.'

'Then don't blame me,' retorted Melinda. 'Blame his guilty conscience.'

'I should hold you entirely to blame.'

'*I* didn't drug myself! *I* didn't rape—'

'Mrs. Gregory,' said Cellini in his coldest voice, 'you are a congenital liar. I have so much evidence of that that I can prove it to the satisfaction of any authority, including coroner, judge and jury. I tell you now that if anything happens to Dr. Selwin, or if you ever make this charge against him, I shall never cease working to prove that he has been falsely accused.'

He turned on his heel and strode out, across the dressing-room and into the passage. But he did not go far. He glanced right and left, to make sure no one was near, then turned and walked very softly back to the bedroom door, not realising that he was emulating Maxine Popple's movements of a short time ago. He could see through the gap between the door and the door frame.

Gregory was sitting up, his wife's hand resting gently on his shoulder. There was a silence for a few moments before Gregory said:

'*Are* you lying, Mel?'

'Why should I lie about Jacob?' she asked.

'Never mind the *why* of it. Are you lying?'

She said, 'I never lie.'

'You're the biggest and most convincing liar I've ever

known,' growled Gregory, but there was neither malice nor resentment in his tone. 'But just for once it might come in useful. Just for once we might be able to work together instead of trying to cut each other's throats.'

'Tell me why I shouldn't want to cut your throat,' retorted Melinda, mockingly. 'Just give me one good reason.'

CHAPTER SIXTEEN

Unholy Union

Cellini was torn between the most uncomfortable feeling that he should not be eavesdropping and an overwhelming temptation to know what these two would say. Something of the bitterness between them, even the hatred, showed up in what had already been said yet there was something else, perhaps inevitable between two people who had been married and lived together for so long; it was a kind of camaraderie, and a sense of readiness, in emergency, to work together in any common interest.

'Melinda, what a bitch you are,' Gregory said.

'I think we each know the other's opinion of ourselves,' said Melinda. 'If you are suggesting that I find you more money, after *this* coup, you *must* be crazy.'

After a short silence, Gregory said in a different tone, 'I've never needed money more.'

'For a man who stole three million poundsworth of his wife's possessions you seem to be very badly off.'

Cellini could just see Gregory's face, and the expression on it seemed shocked, even incredulous.

'*I* didn't steal—good God! Do you think *I* fixed the burglary?'

'Dear Robert, I am sure you did,' retorted Melinda in a sugar-sweet tone.

'You must be mad!'

'Don't you think the word "mad" has been overworked between us lately?'

'But—' Gregory almost spluttered; and then he drew back a hissing breath. 'Is *that* the reason for your latest hate campaign? You think I am robbing you?'

'It's one of the reasons, beloved. I just hate the sight, sound and smell of you, into the bargain. But primarily I was mad—there, now I'm at it!—because you swindled me so perfectly. It was an act of genius to persuade me to let you have the money against the art treasures. I really believed that they were worth more than life itself to you. I should have known the only thing worth *any*thing to you is money.'

Sounding shocked, Gregory said, 'I swear to God I know nothing about it. I thought—' he seemed to choke—'*you* were behind it.'

'Don't be a fool,' Melinda said, a new tone creeping into her voice; a puzzled tone. 'I don't need money.'

'I thought—' Gregory began, but his voice trailed off into heavy breathing.

'Well?' Her tone became peremptory. 'What did you think?'

'You—you knew how much they meant to me. My God, I even passed them on to you so that I could keep them here. Apart from *loving* them for their beauty and their rarity, they were of enormous prestige value. I had only to bring some-one home and they assumed at once I was a billionaire.'

'Whereas you often operated on a shoe string,' Melinda replied. But there was no sneer in her voice now.

'I worked on a narrow margin. I always have. And I've gambled on this world coming to its senses one day. When it does, when we stop these bloody wars and riots and hate campaigns and can get on with the business of peace, *then* my chickens will come home to roost. You think you're rich, but when I collect—' Gregory broke off. 'Oh, forget it! I thought you'd arranged the burglary because it was the one way you could hurt me most.'

'I can hurt you,' she said, in a flat voice. 'I can cause you anguish by just drawing a new man across your sights. But I didn't even think of this.'

She fell silent, and all Cellini could hear was their breathing, his was hardly audible, he kept so still. In the pause he had time to turn to the passage door, and make sure no one was near. Dr. Norris would arrive before long, and he wished now that he hadn't sent for the man, he wanted to hear much more of this strange conversation. He went back to the other door, heard the bed creak, and saw Gregory swing his legs from it. There was a huge, pink bump on his forehead, over the right eye, and his nose was swollen, but there was no other sign of injury. He spoke in a very hard voice.

'You swear you didn't arrange this burglary?'

'I did *not*.'

'Then who did?'

Again there was silence, until Melinda spoke in a wondering voice:

'It was someone who knew exactly what we had here.'

'Every damned piece of any value was taken, yes. And it was done when both you and I were beside ourselves. Who the devil—'

'Bob,' interrupted Melinda, 'are you sure you didn't arrange it just to get back at me for my—love affairs?'

'I might have killed an odd lover now and then, but— no, Mel. I didn't do it.'

'The men in the grounds: didn't you have them there so as to scare the wits out of me?'

'I had the house watched when I was away, sometimes, to see what you were up to, and they scared the wits out of the Popples. But the agency I used wouldn't send three or four on the same night.'

'Someone did, last night!' Melinda did not seem affronted, only anxious to get at the truth.

'Perhaps they were spying out the land for the burglary.'

'I don't believe it. They meant to scare me. *And* they did. I thought at first that's what you wanted.'

'I might want to choke the life out of you with my own hands—' There was another catch of breath, another pause, before Gregory went on roughly, 'If I could I'd put a chastity belt on you and keep the key. And I'd keep a surgical knife handy for some neat little castration jobs—my God, you don't know what agonies of mind I've been through. Loving you has been purgatory, almost from the day I met you, but my fantasies of revenge have always been sexual.'

Melinda said huskily, 'You still feel like that?'

'How the hell do you think I feel?' When she didn't answer, Gregory went on roughly, 'If I hadn't been in love with you do you think I would have kept the marriage going all these years?'

'I—I thought you were so concerned about your reputation.'

'Reputation be damned! No one in banking cares about my morals. Why the hell do you think I've been damned near celibate?'

This time, Melinda caught her breath.

'You didn't know I had been?' Gregory marvelled. 'You were so busy with your lovers you didn't ever stop to look at me. Just now and again I've been out and taken a prostitute, but I haven't led any sex life worth calling sex life because I was bloody fool enough to think that sooner or later you'd get over your love of variety. I thought even you would be surfeited, and that one day you'd be satisfied with me.' After another tense-seeming pause he went on in a harder voice, 'Oh, what the hell! If I didn't fix the burglary, who did? If I wasn't trying to drive you mad, was anybody? We'd got to the stage of agreeing that it had to be someone who knew what we'd got, and who—'

Gregory broke off.

Melinda said, 'Jacob.'

'No.'

'Jacob,' she insisted. 'He fits, everywhere.'

'You're talking nonsense.'

'I'm talking sound common sense,' said Melinda in a very positive voice. 'Jacob fits. He's in love with me and yet knows he's never had a chance.'

'What was all that about him raping you?' growled Gregory.

'All I know for certain is that he got up to some very funny stuff when I was under sedation,' said Melinda.

'I would have trusted him with everything.'

'So would I, until I discovered what he was up to.'

'You mean—*he's* deranged?'

'I mean he's been pestering me to divorce you and marry him for years,' said Melinda. 'See how trustworthy he is! And I've said no, no, no. It isn't that I don't like Jacob, but he's no man for me, and in any case to have a love affair with one's doctor doesn't seem to me a very good idea. Bob—'

'What?'

'How have *you* got on with Jacob?'

'I—well, all right.'

'Has he helped you?'

'He's put me to sleep a lot of times, he—' There was a pause and then a snort of a laugh. 'Don't suppose he's been up to any funny tricks with *me*, do you?'

'Give him credit for *some* good taste,' Melinda retorted, and suddenly, unexpectedly, they both laughed. Soon, Melinda went on, 'Has he been putting us against each other? Am I, in his opinion, insane?'

'You are in need of psychiatric treatment.'

'Would you believe it—you are, too!'

'He always told me so,' said Gregory, almost lamely.

'He told me I did, too, but mostly he said you were insane. He warned me that you would probably kill me in an outburst of violence one day. *My God!* He was always saying how violent you were.'

'Melinda.'

'What?'

'Did you confide in him about your lovers?'

'Confide in *Jacob*?' She sounded astonished.

'Yes.'

'No,' she stated flatly. 'Except—'

'What?'

'I needed pills.'

'Contraceptive pills, you mean?'

'Yes.'

'And he supplied them?'

'Yes.'

'So he knew—' Gregory finished in a kind of gasp.

'I couldn't stop him guessing.'

'But you didn't—you didn't give him the names of—'

'Good heavens, no!'

'Yet—yet he told me.'

'*What?*'

'He told me who some of your lovers were. He told me you were utterly amoral, where sex was concerned, and hadn't the slightest compunction. That—' He broke off.

'Go on,' Melinda said tensely.

'That you preferred young married men because they were less likely to want marriage and you hated marriage like you hate smallpox.'

'Well, well,' breathed Melinda. 'He said all *that*.'

'I thought—'

'You've thought a hell of a lot too much!'

'I thought you told him so that he could pass it on to me, and make life a little more like hell every day.'

'No,' said Melinda. 'I don't know how much he guessed or knew or imagined.' She broke off again, and in the silence which followed there was a kind of breathlessness, or airlessness, which kept Cellini on edge and breathing very softly through his lips. 'I did tell him some things, thinking he was sure to pass them on to you.'

'Such as?'

'Oh—philosophical beliefs.'

'Sex philosophy?'

'Yes.'

'That you believed in free for all where sex was concerned and quoted as your ideal woman the wife of Claudius the First who outlasted all the well-known scarlet women in a frantic succession of lovers.'

'Yes,' said Melinda. 'You—you're such a *bloody* prude.'

'Yes. Could hardly be different, could we? I'm all for one life, one partner, you—oh, forget it! The thing is, Jacob probably hates us both.'

'He—' began Melinda, and this time her voice trailed off.

'In this moment of truth let us have everything,' said Gregory. 'To my surprise it's not hurting as much as I thought it would. It will probably catch up with me later, like a delayed action bomb. He what?'

'He could have had his fun with me because he hated me. Love turning to hate is common, as our nice little Manny Cellini would probably tell us. And Jacob would probably think *I* wouldn't want his antics to become known, so he would feel quite safe. Bob—how can we find out?'

After a pause, Gregory said, 'We could give the police a few broad hints.'

'That *delicious* Superintendent Hardy!'

'No doubt you will offer him your couch when the party is over,' Gregory said, in a voice which suddenly held much hurt. 'Could we discuss this in terms other than your love life?'

As Gregory said that, Cellini was strangely reminded of Jacob Selwin. It was easy to believe that Gregory was as stricken as Selwin had been. How sensitive, how emotional, how fragile even the toughest human males were when confronted by a woman who mattered to them. He himself was much more relaxed now, and deeply pleased, for he understood so much more than he had, and once he could place his knowledge against the proper background, would probably be able to help John Hardy a great deal.

'Bob,' Melinda said in as gentle a tone as she had yet used, 'you read sex into everything I say. Superintendent Hardy *is* delicious. He's like a great big cuddly bear. But even *I* don't mean I want to go to bed with a man because I say he's delicious, or even sexy or bedworthy. You're far too sensitive, my pet.'

Gregory grunted.

'That's neither here nor there. How can we check up on Jacob? Think the police might get a lead from him?'

'Not the police,' Melinda interrupted. 'They would only think we were being vindictive and trying to distract attention from ourselves. But I'll tell you someone whom we *could* put on to Jacob, and who could tell the police for us.'

'Who?'

'Your sweet Dr. Cellini.'

'That's one way of describing him,' said Gregory, gruffly. 'That man is made of steel, don't make any mistake about it. But you're probably right. He's downstairs somewhere, he came here with me. What makes you so sure he'd be the right man?'

'Because he has the police in his pocket, he's a professional friend of Jacob, and he's one of the few men who doesn't ogle me whenever he sets eyes on me. If you were a woman, Bob, you'd sometimes think that all men can see are breasts, buttocks, legs and potential!' She gave a little laugh that was almost gay, and went on, 'He sent for a doctor to look after you, let's wait until the doctor's been, and then—'

'I don't need a doctor!'

'You do, if it's only for your forehead and your nose,' Melinda retorted.

Before she could go on, there were sounds outside in the passage, and Cellini suddenly began to hurry away, reaching the passage before Melinda reached the bedroom door. Turning from the stairs was Popple with a tall, grey-haired, austere man, Dr. Norris.

Now Cellini was in an acute dilemma.

Should he go and see Jacob Selwin immediately, or should he wait until the Gregorys had talked to him? He was badly worried about Selwin: on the other hand he was fascinated by the Gregorys and, in anticipation, by what they would say to him.

All these things were flooding his mind as he went to welcome Norris.

CHAPTER SEVENTEEN

Accusation

Dr. Norris had left, seen off courteously by Cellini.

Robert Gregory's bump had swollen perceptibly and Popple had gone to a chemist to get a prescription made up. Melinda and Gregory were still upstairs, and as Cellini approached from the front door, Maxine Popple came down the stairs.

'Oh, Dr. Cellini!'

'Yes, Mrs. Popple?'

'Mr. and Mrs. Gregory would very much like to see you, before you go.'

'Thank you. Will they come down here?'

'I'm sure they would like you to go up to Mrs. Gregory's apartment, sir.'

'Then I will. I—'

Cellini paused as the telephone rang. Mrs. Popple picked up the receiver on a table on which had stood a Dresden figurine of quite remarkable delicacy.

'The Gregory residence,' she stated, and after only a moment, turned round. 'Yes, he's here. For you, Dr. Cellini.'

Cellini picked up the telephone, half-expecting to hear Hardy, and Hardy it was. Cellini gave himself a moment for preparation, for his head was still humming with what he had heard upstairs; sooner or later he would have to tell Hardy all of it. The pause also gave Mrs. Popple a chance to move away, but she went with some reluctance, as if she would very much like to hear what he said to Hardy.

'Hallo, Superintendent,' he said aloud.

'Manny, what's this about Selwin?'

'It's a little complicated,' answered Cellini, 'but it could be dangerous.'

'You're really sure about that, are you?'

'Yes. I think there is a very real chance that he will attempt to take his own life.'

'Being a doctor, that wouldn't be difficult,' Hardy remarked. 'Do you think he's involved with the robbery?'

'I think he could be, and is in a very precarious position, John, and—'

'He's at home,' Hardy announced.

'Ah.'

'The only way we can prevent him from doing anything there is by interviewing him at his home or taking him away for questioning.'

'Interview him somewhere, I beg you,' said Cellini. 'Preferably at his home. You can appear to be checking on his knowledge of the Gregory family. I hope to go and see him within the hour.'

After a few moments, Hardy said, 'All right, Manny. Are you getting anywhere?'

'I think so, yes. With the people concerned, at all events.'

'What we need is to get somewhere with the thieves,' said Hardy, gruffly. 'I hate to admit it, but we're as far away as ever.' He rang off on that gloomy note, and Cellini put down the receiver as Mrs. Popple appeared from behind a pillar not far away. Well, one could not blame her for being curious, and she had an excellent excuse.

'If you'll follow me, sir.'

She led the way up the stairs, as if Cellini had no knowledge of the layout at all. She went to Melinda Gregory's room and tapped; Gregory appeared almost at once.

'Come in.' His voice was stilted and a little over-hearty. 'Darling! It's Dr. Cellini.'

He glanced round as Melinda came forward quickly, her hand outstretched. It was almost as if she were pretending that she had never seen Cellini before, and had not talked so freely.

'Dr. Cellini, do come in. Maxine, bring some coffee, please.' Chairs stood about a small oval table. A comfortable one was placed for Cellini, who allowed himself to be ushered towards it, refused cigarettes, remarked on the weather, and looked from the man to the woman.

Each was much calmer than when he had last seen them. Melinda was lightly made-up, more for the country than for town, and wore a loose-weave suit of a mauvish-blue shade. Gregory looked a little odd, with the shining lump on his forehead and his swollen nose. Cellini wondered what they would think if they knew he had heard all of their conversation. He wondered, also, what they would think if he allowed for the possibility that each had lied to the other; certainly on their record there was no reason to trust either.

'Dr. Cellini,' began Melinda.

'Dr. Cell—' began Gregory.

'Sorry.'

'No, you go on.'

'I—'

'All right, I will,' said Gregory, looking a little diffident. 'Dr. Cellini, we're in a very delicate position.'

'And only you can help us,' put in Melinda.

'We both hope very much that you will,' went on Gregory.

'I most certainly will if I can,' said Cellini obligingly.

'Thank you.'

'You're very good,' said Gregory. 'Dr. Cellini, we are very troubled about Dr. Selwin. We've known him for many years and have had absolute faith in him but we've discovered some rather disturbing facts, and we don't know how to cope with the situation.'

Was the rape accusation coming? wondered Cellini.

'Very disturbing,' Melinda remarked. 'And partly our fault.'

'The truth is, we know that he has misled each of us about the other,' said Gregory. 'And there is a lot to suggest that he has set out deliberately to put us against each other.'

He paused long enough for Cellini to say, 'It seems most unlikely.'

'Yet it's almost certainly true,' said Melinda. 'Dr. Cellini—'

'Will you try to find out why?' asked Gregory quickly. 'We feel we must find out. The burglary here has been most distressing and—well, we feel that we should know all the facts about everyone who could possibly have played any part in it.'

'You are not seriously suggesting that Dr. Selwin did.'

'It is because we are so anxious not to allow any scandal to spread that we are appealing to you,' Melinda put in. 'If we were to tell the police, they would jump to the conclusion that we were hinting that Dr. Selwin was involved, and that is the last thing we want to imply, even though he could have helped the thieves by giving them information. That's only guesswork. He had the opportunity. On the other hand he has certainly misled us about each other. There must be a reason and we both feel that we must find out why.'

'Will you find out?' asked Gregory, earnestly.

'It would be such a help,' Melinda urged, 'and it would relieve us of a great deal of anxiety. Of course—' She broke off.

'Of course, what?' inquired her husband.

'I was simply going to say that we know this is a professional assignment as it would mean studying Jacob closely, and we would expect Dr. Cellini to charge an appropriate fee. And we know it is a very delicate matter and might take considerable time.'

Money is no object, Cellini thought wryly, but he gave no indication of his feelings as he responded.

'I need to discuss the case with Dr. Selwin, and I will bear all you say in mind. I must ask you one very direct question, however.'

'What do you want to know?' asked Gregory.

'Do you suspect Dr. Selwin of any part in the burglary?'

There was an awkward pause, before Melinda said, 'I can't really believe it.'

'We've known him so long,' said Gregory, evasively.

'But he has lied to us—' put in Melinda.

'About one another—' Gregory's words were a refrain.

'I will most certainly try to find out the truth,' said Cellini. 'You would help me considerably in this if you would confirm—or deny—a statement by him to the effect that you frequently stationed men—private detectives—in the grounds to watch your wife. Is that true?'

Gregory turned red very slowly, and looked at Melinda as he answered, 'Yes, I did. I hired an agency and gave them *carte blanche* to watch when and as they liked. They reported to me only if they had reason to suspect that someone was with my wife. But you kept the house sweet and pure, didn't you, Melinda?'

'I certainly didn't bring boy-friends here,' Melinda retorted.

At that moment Mrs. Popple came in with coffee.

'Thank you, thank you,' Cellini said, 'but I really shouldn't stay. This matter could be very urgent.' He gave them all his rather shy, yet charming smile and went towards the door. As Gregory followed, he went on, 'Thank you, I can find my own way out. I am becoming most familiar with this lovely house.'

But Gregory stayed by his side, walking almost mincingly

to keep pace with Cellini's shorter stride.

'Dr. Cellini, please understand one thing.'

'What particular thing, Mr. Gregory?'

'Dr. Selwin is a very old friend of mine.'

'So I understand.'

'If I can help him in any way—' Gregory waved his hands as if hardly knowing how to finish.

'I shall in any case want to help a friend and colleague as much as possible,' Cellini said, a note of reproof in his voice.

Gregory waved his hands again, then let them fall by his side. They went down the central staircase together, Gregory going ahead to open the front door, which was now closed. A blast of cold air came in, carrying a few spots of rain. Cellini shivered, involuntarily.

'Cellini,' Gregory said abruptly, 'if you can help Selwin I'll be damned grateful. If you can help to find the missing art treasures I shall forever be in your debt.'

Cellini nodded, and went out to the hired car. With almost embarrassing solicitude, Gregory followed him and opened the driving door. Rain stood in tiny globules on the shiny black surface of the hired car, an Austin 1100. The engine started at the first touch, and Cellini eased off the clutch and moved forward as smoothly as if he had been driving this modern car for months. He did not see Gregory go back into the house.

He drove slowly for a while, trying to assimilate all he had heard and to see it in its proper perspective. He needed more time, as indeed he did in most of his cases, in which to reflect, to see all sides of each question; and this case was much more difficult than most. There was the need to balance what Melinda Gregory had said in her different moods, with what Gregory had said. Any one conversation could give a completely false impression. Melinda in a vicious, malevolent mood, seemed only a thorough-going bitch, but at times there was a softness and gentleness about her which showed surprisingly. He needed not minutes, not even hours, but days in which to consider and ponder, and there was a grave danger of making a serious mistake if he did not allow enough time.

Much suggested, however, that there might be little time in which to deal with Selwin.

He drove past the pond and then turned left, towards the other part of Hampstead Heath, in which Selwin lived. His house was one of an early-Victorian terrace, steps led up to each porticoed porch; others led to the basement and the kitchen quarters. Most of these houses had been turned into small, exclusive and expensive flats, but Selwin had a whole house to himself, for he had young children as well as a grown-up family. A policeman was strolling on one side of the street, no doubt keeping the house under observation. A woman with red hair was pushing a double pram out of the front gateway as Cellini pulled up.

Her face brightened.

'Hallo, Dr. Cellini!'

'Hallo, Mrs. Selwin! How are you?'

'Oh, I'm fine.'

'And so are the twins, obviously.'

The twins, almost too large for the pram and not far off the walking stage, were round and red-faced, plump and bright-eyed. They regarded Cellini with owlish interest and he made appropriate signs and gestures while speaking to their mother.

'Is Jacob in?'

'Yes. He's with someone from Scotland Yard.'

'Oh, dear. What a business it all is.'

'I wish to goodness it had never happened!'

'We all do,' murmered Cellini. 'Is Jacob very worried by it?'

'He's worried out of his life!'

'Why does it trouble him so much?' asked Cellini.

'He's been worried about both the Gregorys for a long time,' she answered, 'and he felt that this could *really* drive them round the bend. I don't mean—' she began hastily.

'It's all right,' Cellini assured her. 'This is just between ourselves. And I know how he feels about the Gregory family, too. Is there any other reason for his being so worried?'

'No.' Clear and attractive brown eyes clouded for a moment, and then she went on, 'No, not really. But he's been very troubled lately, much more than he used to be. He seems to consider each patient's problems as his own.'

'Including the Gregorys?'

'Especially the Gregorys!'

'Isn't he sleeping well?' inquired Cellini.

'I don't think he would sleep at all without his tablets,' Mrs. Selwin replied, with obvious feeling. 'Please help him if you can.'

'I most certainly will,' promised Cellini. 'No, don't come with me, I'd rather ring the bell myself.'

She nodded, and he went up the steps, past the portico of past splendours to the black-painted front door. He rang the bell marked *Private*, and waited only for a few seconds before a young woman in a plain navy blue dress, somehow decorous although it showed so much of her attractive legs, opened the door.

'Dr. Selwin, please,' Cellini said.

'I'm sorry, sir—'

'Tell Dr. Selwin I'm here,' ordered Cellini. 'My name is Cellini.'

'Dr. Cellini!' She was suddenly excited, and obviously delighted. 'Please do come in, Dr. Selwin will be free in a few minutes. *Do* come in.' She led the way, hips flaunting, long shapely legs a temptation. She led him by a route which meant that he did not see the Yard man. Soon he was in a small waiting room. The door between that and the consulting room was closed, although he could hear voices.

'No, I have no idea,' Selwin was saying.

'But you must have seen him,' protested another voice. 'It isn't that we are doubting your word, simply that we must have a description of the man who appeared at the window. I—' A bell sounded, and Selwin said simply, 'I must answer that. It is urgent.'

'What can be of such vital importance?' demanded the man with him, obviously a policeman.

'I have a lot of patients and some are on the danger list,' said Selwin. 'This might be from ... Hallo. Who? Oh, you will. I told you I was busy ... Oh. Is he.' There was a scrape of chair legs, obviously Selwin getting to his feet. His voice came again, 'I'm sorry, I can't spare any more time. I have to see a consultant. Dr. Cellini. If I can be of use tomorrow please let me know.'

His companion made little demur. There was the opening and closing of a door, and then quiet. Cellini expected the other to appear, but he did not; obviously there was a side door. There were little sounds, no more, and these must have some significance or Jacob Selwin would have come straight to the waiting-room. Cellini hesitated, less in impatience than in anxiety, then decided he could wait no longer. He strode forward and thrust the door open.

As it opened, Selwin spun round from a hand-basin. He had tablets in one hand, a glass of water in the other. His lips were parted when he saw Cellini. He thrust the tablets to his mouth and threw back his head in an effort to swallow them, lifting the glass to his lips. Cellini was too far away to prevent this, but a small table with a telephone and some bottles was close to the door. He snatched a bottle up and hurled it at Selwin. It struck the hand holding the glass.

The glass dropped, water spraying in all directions, and Selwin began to cough and splutter. Cellini seized his left arm in a hammerlock and bent him backwards, then thrust the fingers of his other hand into Selwin's mouth.

Selwin choked; coughed almost in a spasm; and had just time to reach the hand-basin before he was sick.

That was all that Cellini wanted, for he must have brought up whatever tablets he had swallowed. He was still coughing and spluttering while Cellini eased him into a wooden armchair and placed another glass of water at his lips.

Soon, Selwin began to sip.

CHAPTER EIGHTEEN

Confession

'What did you take?' asked Cellini, briskly.

'Strychnine,' answered Selwin, hoarsely.

'Painful for you and distressing for your wife and everyone else.'

'It was nearest and quickest,' said Selwin hoarsely.

Cellini gave him a little more time to recover before going on. It was ten minutes since the furious outburst of violence, and although he sounded so hoarse Selwin had recovered from the bout of coughing, and the tears brought on by the coughing had stopped. The original glass, unbroken, now stood on a small desk where Cellini sat; Selwin was sitting in the wooden armchair usually used by his patients. He looked badly shaken and his eyes were glassy. By his side was a tray of coffee, made in a tiny alcove leading from the surgery.

'Perhaps you can answer me something, Manny,' Selwin said. 'Where does thinking end and feeling begin?'

'You know as well as I do that they often overlap,' answered Cellini. 'How long have you been in love with Melinda Gregory?'

'For much longer than she's been married.'

'Did you tell her so before she was married?'

'No. I was married then, and I've been divorced and married again since. She knew I was in love with her before both of my marriages but she was very positive that there wasn't a chance for me. She—' He brushed his hand across his eyes. 'She made it clear that she was living the life she wanted. Safely anchored to Robert Gregory, she could do what she liked, have as many *affaires* as she liked, without becoming involved in another permanent liaison. Her marriage to Bob was never really a marriage, of course. They seldom slept together, even in the early days. God knows why he stuck it, but something made him.'

Cellini made no comment.

'I thought she was crazy to keep on with the marriage,' said Selwin. 'I still think she is. But—' He broke off. 'I didn't realise how cruel she could be.'

'Cruel?' echoed Cellini, as if he did not understand.

'Yes. She wanted me to find a way of proving that Bob is insane. When I refused she tried to blackmail me.' He pressed the palms of his hands against his eyes. 'And she persuaded Maxine Popple to help her. You would never believe—'

'I know exactly what she did,' said Cellini, mercifully.

'You *know*? How can you?' There was a change of tone, to anger, in Selwin's voice.

'People talk much more freely than they realise,' Cellini said. 'Jacob, how true is her story that you first put her under sedation and then had intercourse with her?'

Selwin's eyes were burning.

'It's not true.'

'But Maxine Popple is prepared to confirm it.'

'Yes,' muttered Selwin. 'I know she is.'

'Jacob,' Cellini said softly. 'You just tried to kill yourself. That is presumably because she made this accusation and you could not face the story if it came out. You would be struck off the General Medical Register and be ruined. However, if the whole thing was a trumped up lie, you would hardly have taken such a drastic step so quickly. The time has come to tell someone the whole truth. If I know it, I may be able to help.'

'Suppress such a story? *You?*'

'Of course, unless I thought it was something the police should know, or which would interfere with your carrying out your duties as a physician. What *is* the truth, Jacob?'

Selwin was silent for what seemed a very long time, and his expression was one of near despair. He looked so old; had aged ten years since he had first introduced Cellini to the Gregorys. He tried to speak several times, but could not; and Cellini waited, making no attempt to prompt him. At last, he managed to speak coherently although his voice was low and hoarse.

'I've never—raped her. I have—removed her dress. Not—absolutely. She—she often wore nothing under her blouse or dress. At most—a flimsy brassière. I—I often saw her when she was in bed. I—I have pulled her blouse off her shoulders, and—removed the bra. She is—so beautiful. I sometimes thought I would go mad if I could not touch her. And—touching her soothed me. Calmed me. I—I did not need to—to do more than fondle her. I—I knew it was crazy. I was so tempted to go further but I never allowed myself to. I've never—never felt like it with any woman before. Just to sit there and look at her would mean more to me than—than making love to my wife, or—' He broke off, and his eyes were full of tears and pain. 'It became—became a habit. I almost wanted her—I *did* want her—to need sedation. My need for her began to possess me. But I never went further. I did not touch her below—below the waist. For some strange reason, I had no desire to. I had no fantasies about possessing her absolutely; seeing and touching her was enough. It was a kind of perfection, a dream come true. You see, her—her lovers had her body. And no one who simply wanted to lie with her could possibly get the pleasure, the ecstasy that I got from touching her breasts, her waist, her throat.

'Then, one day—Maxine Popple saw me.'

Selwin broke off, screwed up his eyes and raised his hands as if to fend off some invisible creature. He was silent for a long time, his mouth working, and at last he burst out, 'She came in, and I was bending over Melinda. I am not sure whether she knew what I was doing—my back was in her line of vision. She drew back, apologetically, said she'd thought I'd gone, and turned away. She gave me an old-fashioned look when I left that day, and I didn't stay so long after that, but it wasn't until today that Melinda told me that she'd seen what I was doing. The rape story was an elaboration. Maybe what I did was as bad in its way, pro-fessionally it was unforgivable, and—'

'Jacob, *did* you ever make love to Melinda when she was unconscious?'

'No, I did not.'

'Have you ever made love to her, with her compliance?'

'No. Never.'

'Then why did you attempt to commit suicide?'

'Surely you can understand,' said Selwin, almost angrily. 'I could never touch her again. One of my reasons for living would be gone. And if that weren't enough, there would be the scandal. If Melinda made the charge and Maxine Popple corroborated it, I wouldn't have a chance. There would be a long period of waiting before the General Medical Council heard the charges and they would certainly decide to strike me off the medical register. Apart from the ordeal for myself, my wife would go through hell. If I killed myself there would be rumours but there would be no charges. My wife is younger than I, and she would soon remarry, probably much more happily. As it is—I don't know whether to be grateful or to hate you for coming when you did.'

'It is immaterial,' Cellini declared. 'We have the problem of Melinda and Robert Gregory on our hands and they are

our main responsibility. How much did they—or do they—
hate each other?'

'Sometimes they could kill each other,' stated Selwin,
quite positively. 'At others they seemed to rub along. It's a
love-hate relationship, I suppose. They can't live with each
other and they can't live without each other, or they think
they can't.'

'You think they could,' murmured Cellini.

'Yes, of course. They'd have a far better chance of leading
happy lives separately.'

'Melinda, no doubt, with you,' Cellini said slyly.

'No,' said Selwin, heavily. 'Oh, I once dreamed of that,
but never very realistically. We might make good lovers,
but I don't think we could live together happily. Melinda
needs someone quite different. In fact,' he went on heavily,
'I'm not sure she wouldn't live most happily on her own.
She seems to need a kind of protective screen, and Bob is
that screen. Or marriage is. It enables her—' He gave a
brief, bitter laugh. 'It enables her to be more selective.'

At last, his words seemed to dry up.

He poured himself some lukewarm coffee and drank it
with apparent enjoyment, put his cup down and squared his
shoulders. He looked so much better, there was even brightness in his eyes.

'Well, Manny! Wasn't suicide the simplest way out?'

'For you, possibly,' answered Cellini, 'but certainly not
for anyone else. Jacob, have you ever behaved like this over
any other patient?'

'I have not.'

'Or been tempted to?'

'No. I am quite detached when examining woman patients,
even the most voluptuous of them.'

'Have you ever had an *affaire* with a patient?'

Selwin smiled faintly. 'Never.'

'Intercourse?'

'I tell you—*never*. I am most punctilious in behaviour, both because I should be and because I want to be. You must know that one becomes almost automatically indifferent.'

'I want to be sure that you do, always.'

'Except for Melinda, yes. And I was in love with her before I left St. Barts, and she was barely in her teens.' Selwin leaned forward. 'Manny, why are you asking these questions?'

'For the best of reasons,' answered Cellini. 'If I had the slightest suspicion that you had a tendency this way, I would certainly have to report it. If it is a matter solely between you and Melinda Gregory, and Melinda doesn't wish to make a complaint, then—'

'You really would keep silent?' Selwin marvelled.

'I should have a battle with my conscience,' replied Cellini, 'and I would have to feel very sure you were not likely ever to be so afflicted again, but I don't think I would feel compelled to report what I have learned today.'

Selwin closed his eyes; and after a few moments, tears squeezed themselves from between the lids, and he gripped the arms of his chair very tightly. Cellini, aware of the slackening tension, gave him a few minutes to recover, and at the same time considered his own attitude. Then, he turned to what had to be faced with the Gregorys and with Hardy; what he had discovered today spread a fascinating light on the personal, emotional problems of three of the people involved, but did nothing to help the police in their main problem.

At last, he said, 'I want to ask you some questions about the Gregorys, Jacob.'

'Go ahead,' Selwin said. He brushed the back of his hand across his forehead and straightened up again.

'Have you heard anything from either of them to suggest they were involved in the burglary?'

'Nothing.'

'Are you sure of that?'

'The treasures themselves are so important to them that I can't believe they would have anything to do with the burglary. It would be absolute sacrilege to them.'

'Except perhaps for highly emotional and personal reasons,' Cellini suggested.

'To hurt one another?' asked Selwin.

'Yes.'

'I may have implied that they would,' said Selwin, 'but I don't seriously think that they would go so far.'

'Has Robert Gregory ever talked about being in need of capital?'

Selwin pondered.

'No, not lately. He's been bitter because Melinda won't put her own and their trust money into his business, but I've no reason to believe he's in any difficulty.'

'Melinda?'

Selwin laughed.

'She's one of the Wolf family—fabulously wealthy.'

'The Wolf family,' mused Cellini. They were, he knew, considered to be rich enough to be far beyond financial temptation. It was almost impossible to believe that a branch of the Wolfs could ever become involved in theft, though they could easily become hopelessly involved with other people's affairs. Unless Gregory had in fact incurred some heavy losses, then neither of them could have been involved in the burglary for gain.

For revenge perhaps?

Cellini fingered his moustache, and then asked with an air of finality:

'You are absolutely sure that neither has been in money trouble?'

'I'm simply sure I haven't the slightest reason to believe that either has been or is likely to be seriously in trouble over money,' replied Selwin. Then for the first time since Cellini had arrived he smiled. 'Manny, you haven't ruled out the possibility that this was a simple robbery for gain, have you? There *are* art thieves, and there are big markets for these treasures. This may be a case for Hardy and not for a psychiatrist.'

'It could indeed,' said Cellini. 'How wealthy are you, Jacob?'

'I'm not wealthy at all. I'm comfortable—' He broke off. 'Good God! You don't think that I—' His voice trailed off and he looked at Cellini almost incredulously.

'You could have been involved, after all.'

'Well, I haven't been. I—' Jacob gulped. 'I couldn't understand why the police kept on asking me questions! And now you—what the devil's got into you? Do you think I've been so warped in my mind that I want to hurt them because they've hurt me emotionally?'

'It *is* possible,' said Cellini, almost defensively.

'Oh, yes, it's possible,' said Selwin. 'And—my God! If I'd killed myself—'

'A great number of people might have regarded it as a confession of guilt.'

'Oh,' said Selwin, and stood up for the first time and glared down at Cellini. 'Go back and tell your policeman friend that he's barking up the wrong tree. I—good *God*! I've never been so bloody angry in my life! And you—*you* actually think it's possible!'

'*All* things are possible,' Cellini said mildly. 'Jacob—'

'For *you* to think—'

'Jacob,' interrupted Cellini sharply, 'a lot of people would find it easier to believe you were involved in the burglary than to believe what you've told me about your attitude towards Melinda. I shouldn't wax so indignant.' When Selwin stopped as if he had come up against a wall, Cellini went on, 'I want you to go back over the past few weeks and recall whether either Melinda or Robert Gregory has said anything to suggest that they might have been driven to take part in such a fraud. Whether either hated the other enough to involve him or her. No, don't say you're quite sure, now. Just think about it. And if you recall anything that could help, let me know at once.'

'Very well,' said Selwin, 'but there isn't the slightest hope that I shall remember anything.'

'Try,' said Cellini. 'For your own sake.'

'*What?*'

'Because if either of them is involved, they might well want to throw the blame on someone else,' Cellini pointed out. 'You would be a very easy one to involve, and after Melinda's readiness to blackmail you, you surely realise that if she wanted a thing badly enough she wouldn't stop at much to get it.'

'No,' agreed Selwin, very slowly. 'No, she certainly wouldn't.'

'If you have heard or been aware of anything to help the police it is somewhere in the back of your mind,' Cellini declared. 'It could be of vital importance, Jacob, to yourself and to either of the others. Now!' He stood up. 'I really must go.'

CHAPTER NINETEEN

Something Remembered

Cellini turned into the driveway of his own apartment about half-past five that afternoon, called the car agency to collect the car, still glad he had not taken his own. He was very tired. He moved slowly, and was a little put out when he had to wait for the lift, but at last he opened the front door of his own apartment, and called:

'Felisa!'

There was no reply.

'*Surely* she isn't out,' he said vexedly.

But she was out, and there was a note in the kitchen saying: '*I will be back at six o'clock.*' Still disgruntled, for he was in conscious need of Felisa's fussing, he made himself some tea, took it into the sitting-room, kicked off his shoes and put his legs up on a pouffe, and drank the tea with relish. Gradually, the physical tiredness faded into a sense almost of well-being. He began to doze, feeling as if he were floating on air. Gradually, faces hovered in front of his eyes, imagined faces. Melinda; Robert Gregory; the Popples; Hardy; Selwin; and most vividly, strangely enough, Selwin's young and pleasant wife.

He studied them all in turn.

In a state of semi-consciousness he marvelled at their behaviour, and even more at the fact that he had become so deeply involved. That was his vocation, of course, to become involved in other peoples' lives and not his own. It was really quite remarkable. And it was easy to forget how extremely lucky he was, with Felisa. He needed her calmness, her love, her readiness to look after his creature comforts in every way. It would be easy to underrate how important she was to him, and how much he depended on her, how unselfishly she subjugated herself to him yet retained a remarkable personality of her own. No, not to him, but to his needs. And look how impatient he had been when, for once, she hadn't been waiting here for him.

She was a remarkable woman.

She was a *very* remarkable woman.

She had made it very obvious that she would not have been troubled if he *had* allowed himself to go further with Melinda Gregory than he should have. Nonsense! But was it nonsense? In his half-dozy frame of mind, he speculated. He really *was* absurd, and Felisa, bless her, must know it. To imagine himself even momentarily as Melinda's paramour—really! What was the matter with him? She had lured him on, of course, not to seduce him but to make fun of him. Foolish old man! And Felisa, when he had told her, had behaved as if such a conquest was in the natural order of things. Ridiculous! Melinda Gregory and he—nonsense. And yet, she *had* enticed him. And he wasn't wholly satisfied that it had been to make fun of him. Then why had she behaved in such a way? Melinda, who *was* really beautiful, who had a superb body, who could bed with any man she chose, for all the evidence showed that she was a sexual profligate. How ludicrous to think that she would have taken him to her. Really! An old man—well, in the middle sixties, comparatively old. Yet he could remember her so vividly. She had invited him. She had made it extremely difficult for him to refuse. Even at this moment it was difficult to understand why he *had* refused.

He felt a stirring in his loins.

Man was man. It was a long time since he had known such moments as these, awareness of sensual desire, as distinct from sexual need. A glow which spread from his loins throughout his body, giving him such a sense of well-being. How strange it was that society had decreed when a man should feel as he felt now. That society had decreed that man and woman could only satisfy this stirring of natural desire in wedlock. Out of wedlock, satisfaction was 'wrong'. Of course, the young people today rejected this. They accepted the mating call for what it was. A moment, though. Not all young people did. Some were still controlled by custom, by their environment, by their training. Seldom if ever by their instincts. But what *was* the truth? Society did need some restraint. It was all very difficult. Yet he, Emmanuel Cellini, had seen more people with disturbed psyches than most, and he knew—in common with all of his professional colleagues—that the foundation of nearly all emotional disturbances in the human animal was sexual. Sexual frustration, in one form or another.

But back to the immediate problem!

He actually opened his eyes and sat up, but soon he drooped again; the late night of the previous day was now taking its toll. His mind was clear, thanks be. The immediate problem, he had to admit, was a confused one with three facets.

Help Melinda.

Help Gregory.

Help Jacob Selwin.

Oh, yes, and there was the other one: help the police.

He could not do much more for Jacob, but had to make a very delicate decision. He would have to satisfy himself that there was no danger of Jacob responding to another woman as he did to Melinda.

Melinda.

He had not seen Melinda as Jacob had, but he could

imagine her almost hypnotic—no, magnetic; no, mesmeric—
effect. So he had to come back to his original train of
thought about Melinda. She had tempted him, it had been
almost irresistible, but supposing he *had* been a lecherous
old man. Supposing he *had* gone to bed with her, or attempted to.

Why did 'attempted to' spring to his mind?

On the surface of the situation which he saw so vividly,
there was no question of attempting, the invitation had been
so natural. Yet had it been? What was going on in his mind,
what was he thinking? Had she really been ready to lie with
him? Had she? Was it possible that she had known that he
would discipline himself, and show sufficient self-control to
stay away from her bed?

He stirred again. The desire in his loins had gone, the
glow in his body with it; now his mind was as clear and alert
as he had ever known it. Different thoughts, scintillas of
thought, were bombarding him from all directions. His body
was asleep but his mind was fiercely alive. He was on the
borderline of some new understanding; a kind of revelation.
The 'flash' as some philosophers called it, the moment when
a single flash illuminated the dark corners of the mind and
revealed a host of things which had been shrouded in darkness. He was hardly breathing.

*Would she have taken him to her bed, or had she simply
pretended to seduce him?*

*Had she meant what she had said, or simply been trying
to convince him with her brazenness, her readiness to allow
anyone to be with her?*

*If she pretended with him, had she pretended about
others?*

*Had she wanted to convince him of her own promiscuity,
to reveal herself the creature of her reputation?*

There was the flash; the first flash, which died at once.

He had not seen what he wanted to see but he was aware of vague shapes, vague possibilities in his mind.

If she put on such an act with him, had she with her husband? And Selwin?

There were things to remember.

She had never slept with Jacob Selwin; had she done there would have been no need for his particular form of fetishism. Yet he was a handsome man, and undoubtedly virile. He had known her for years. The opportunities for lovemaking had been glaringly obvious and frequent, yet she had done nothing to encourage it.

And although Gregory had employed private inquiry agents to watch the house, on his own statement there had been no adultery at *Hethersett*.

And—she had behaved like a bitch. If he had known her without any foreknowledge of her sexual life, he would have thought simply that she was sexually deprived; sex-starved. He would have assumed that her—no, he would have assumed nothing. He would have considered the possibility that her husband was impotent, or else homosexual, and that she had no normal sex-life and so behaved like a shrew. Sex-deprivation *was* a common cause of bitchy behaviour. But he had also to remember that Robert Gregory had not behaved like an impotent man, rather like a man denied the usual and the necessary sexual activity. Some turned homosexual, some to masturbation, some to prostitutes or to any woman who was compliant, others simply drove the desire within themselves away. And this had the same effect on a man as sexual starvation had on a woman. Studying the Gregorys both from what he knew of them and what Selwin had told him, they lived cat-and-dog, and the commonest cause of such a life *was* sexual frustration.

Two frustrated people, man and wife.

But—how could such a woman as Melinda be frustrated? In his experience women of the temperament to get their satisfaction from a variety of men were *not* frustrated. They were more likely to be happy than unhappy. In the beginning, when fighting down the almost inevitable guilt complex in the early days, they had problems and lashed about a bit, but once they had come to terms with their own nature then they were comparatively tranquil. He knew a surprising number of women who ran very happy households and kept their husbands wholly satisfied, sexually, while drawing their own contentment from lovers who made no extra-sexual demands on them. He had even heard it argued that there was a case for houses of assignation for women, but his own feeling was that society had to find some way of enabling its members to be happy in daily life, not to have houses of assignation for women, or brothels for men. There was something basically and drastically wrong with society, particularly the attitude towards sex, but his, Cellini's, task was to help people within the existing society.

Individuals were often in desperate need of help.

Like Melinda Gregory.

He realised that he was much calmer than he had been, and surprisingly tired; he had reached a point of knowledge. He now knew the truth about one thing, and although it might surprise many people, including Selwin, he could see it clearly as a major part of the explanation of the problem.

Melinda Gregory did *not* have a swift succession of lovers.

Melinda Gregory had little if any sex life.

And such deprivation would not only explain much of her attitude and behaviour but it would also explain her obvious conviction that Selwin first drugged and then raped her. The sexually frustrated had the most vivid fantasies, and given the slightest basis for a fantasy they would build it up. In this case, of course, Melinda's fantasy had been fed by Maxine Popple who was probably one of the few people who had reason to suspect that Melinda's sexual promiscuity was imaginary, not real. And no one who had met the

Popples could doubt that they were pro-Melinda and anti-Robert. It was apparent that they would do everything they could to ease life for her, pamper, pet and spoil her. And in so doing they could only have created the conditions which worsened Gregory's standing as master of the household.

It was difficult to know whether to be sorry most for Melinda or for Robert Gregory.

Cellini stopped active thinking. His body and his mind were at ease, now, as if both were resting after a period of excessive activity. And in a way that was true, of course; he had been wildly active. However, he could not rest for long. There was the other, acute problem: of the burglary. Hardy would work ceaselessly at that, and one of the main possibilities was that Gregory had connived at the burglary to collect the insurance; another, that Melinda had connived at it out of a form of revenge against her husband.

But what if neither was true?

There was a sound in the distance. A bell. He did not want to be disturbed. But there was a bell. It rang and rang. So it was the telephone bell. He did not want— It stopped.

He heard a voice.

Goodness, was Felisa back?

He opened his eyes wider and sat up. The door opened and Felisa appeared, moving very slowly until she saw that he was awake. She said softly:

'It was John Hardy, Manny.'

'Who?' He was wool-gathering.

'John. John Hardy.'

'Oh,' he said. 'John. Yes. I will come.'

'He is coming here,' she told him. 'You need not disturb yourself. Sit there and I will bring you some tea.'

'But I *have* some tea!'

'Nonsense,' Felisa said, fondly. 'You let that go cold. I came in and fetched the tray half-an-hour ago. I was glad to see you sleeping. You needed a good rest.'

Sleep, echoed Cellini to himself, feeling most indignant. 'I have never been wider awake or more alert! Asleep indeed!'

But Felisa had gone and he eased his cramped legs and then looked at his watch—goodness! It was seven o'clock. He had been home for at least three hours. Well, well. He had been tuned in to his subconscious mind while asleep, then. He had known it happen before, but not often. Remarkable!

What did Hardy want?

Felisa brought in his tea and some chocolate biscuits, and would not stay with him. She was preparing dinner. Hardy wasn't due yet, so there was ten minutes before he, Manny, need bestir himself. He enjoyed the hot tea and was completely alert and moving about when Hardy arrived.

He looked urbane and immaculate, and yet perhaps just a little harassed and warm.

'Hallo, Manny.' He mopped his flushed face. 'Sorry to intrude just before dinner, but I wanted to ask you one specific question which isn't easy over the telephone.'

'I am very glad to see you. Do sit down. And won't you stay—'

'No, Felisa has already asked me.'

'Then a drink? Your favourite whisky and soda?'

'Just what I need!' As Cellini began to get out glasses and decanter, Hardy leaned back in the armchair where Robert Gregory had once dozed, and went on, 'I'm puzzled by one thing, Manny, and it's really in your department. I put a man on to checking Melinda Gregory's boy friends, because any one of them might have had a chance to case the house, as it were. And he's come up with a block buster.'

Cellini turned round, decanter in one hand, glass in the other.

'No boy friends,' he remarked, innocently.

'*What?*'

'Your block buster is that she has few if any boy friends. She has lived a life of fantasy for most of her marriage. Isn't that it?' Cellini carried the whisky and a soda syphon to Hardy. 'You see—we arrive at the same conclusion by different routes.'

'So it *is* true,' Hardy said. 'We checked on four of her supposed lovers, and came to the conclusion that they were no more than friends. Two are out of the country most of the time. And you suspected this?'

'Quite recently I had reason to suspect,' replied Cellini.

'Well I'm damned. Thanks.' Hardy drank. '*Ahh!* I needed that.' He looked very hard at Cellini as he went on, 'I should have known you would get to it. Did you talk to the private inquiry agents whom Gregory employed?'

'Most certainly not!'

'Well, we did,' said Hardy. 'And they'd collected practically no indications. They didn't give Gregory the full reports because it would have killed the goose who laid the golden eggs. In fact one of their partners said it was almost as if Gregory *wanted* to believe she was a whore.' Hardy paused again, and gulped. 'The one frequent visitor with whom there might have been some evidence, was Dr. Selwin. And he could be involved in the burglary. I've had his movements traced and he doesn't appear to have made any new acquaintances lately. Unless you've discovered anything—' He broke off, hopefully.

'I think Selwin is quite free from suspicion,' Cellini told him.

'So, one or the other of the Gregorys has been playing fast and loose with us.' Hardy finished his drink in two gulps, and sat upright. 'Manny, I know you are in a semi-professional capacity with both. I know all about a doctor not betraying his patient's confidences. However, this is a major art theft, and it could have considerable repercussions. We have had no luck at all in tracing the van in which the goods were removed. No one has put them, or any single item, on the market yet—not a single one. All ships and aircraft leaving the country have been checked, and terminals in Europe have been alerted to watch for the items in the collection. We worked on the possibility that the thieves would get everything out of the country quickly, and didn't lose a minute. The truth is, however, that the loot has vanished, and we haven't a clue. The newspapers are getting fractious, and between you and me, so are my superiors. Now if you've made any discovery which might point to either of the Gregorys, I want to know—quickly.'

Cellini moved across and picked up Hardy's glass.

'I would tell you, John, but neither of them has given me the slightest indication. However—' He broke off as he replenished the glass, and spoke again as he carried it towards Hardy. 'There is one other possibility I am sure you have considered. You would be bound to reach it by a process of elimination, and I have no doubt it came to your mind almost as a reflex, although I reached it by the accumulation of what I call psychological evidence.'

He finished as he placed the glass in Hardy's hand.

Hardy was smiling.

'Elimination?' he repeated. 'The obvious suspects, mostly disregarded at first because they were so obvious.'

'Yes,' confirmed Cellini. 'The one certain thing is that the thieves had to know exactly what was worth taking, the kind of fixtures and fastenings. They even distinguished between modern and old Mirzapore carpets. So they had ample time to study and assess the value, and could only have had such opportunities by being here often, or—'

'Living here,' Hardy finished for him. 'The Popples.'

'Precisely,' said Cellini mildly. 'The Popples. Are you sure you won't stay to dinner and then come over with me to see them? I would very much like to be in on the final act,' he added, a glint in his eyes.

Hardy said, 'Thanks. Yes, I'd like to. And they were the reflex suspects we didn't really want to believe in.' He picked up his glass, and toasted, 'To the guilt of the Popples,' and drank deeply.

CHAPTER TWENTY

Shock

'What put you on to them?' asked Hardy. 'And are you sure? We're not, yet.'

'I cannot be positive,' Cellini said, 'but it does look extremely likely. As for how I came to the conclusion—well, it was a matter of evidence, or at least of indications. They had such opportunities. And they knew that in these wild quarrels, Gregory could easily forget to set the burglar alarm —or they could unset it and say he'd forgotten.'

Cellini stopped. Sitting back in a police car with Hardy by his side, he had a lot of time for reflection. He was to an increasing degree aware of the weakness of his own arguments, and it was difficult to put across the causes for suspicion which could best be expressed in nuances of expression. How, for instance, the Popples had talked afterwards of the men in the grounds; they had not mentioned it until after the event, explaining their strange reticence as being due to the desire not to upset the Gregorys. There had been the 'terror' on the night of the burglary, caused, the Popples had said, by these same men; but they knew that Gregory was having the house watched. Their 'terror', then, must have been faked. There had been their enormous relief after the burlary, too. At a time when their concern for their mistress might have been calculated to make them more distressed, a few hours sleep had worked miracles with them and on the day after the burglary they had behaved as if a great burden had been lifted from their shoulders.

'As indeed it would have been had they been involved in the burglary,' Cellini argued. 'Once it was carried out, they had done their share and could relax. They could feel quite confident, since the men had been seen in the grounds, that it would seem an outside job. They were a different couple after the crime, John.'

'I wouldn't know about that, but I do know you're making sense,' said Hardy. 'We'll soon see. How would you tackle them?' he asked indulgently.

'I've no doubt at all,' said Cellini. 'We must go as if we want to make more inquiries—about Dr. Selwin, preferably, they will be half-prepared to expect you to be suspicious of Selwin—and then I advise you to charge them, out of the blue. One or the other will give something away.'

Hardy said, 'I certainly hope so.'

They turned into the drive of Hethersett ten minutes later, and soon they were in the big, bare room with the Popples. Popple himself looked tired but in no way frightened, and his wife had a very self-assured manner.

'I want to ask you a few questions about the frequency of Dr. Selwin's visits here,' began Hardy. He sat at the desk, the Popples in front of him, Cellini at his side, so inconspicuous that he seemed almost like a dummy. 'How often did Dr. Selwin come, Mrs. Popple?'

'Nearly every day,' she answered promptly.

'Did you ever send for him?'

'Only occasionally,' Popple answered this time. 'But usually he came when he was doing his rounds.'

'Did he spend much time up in their rooms? Or—'

'Most of the time he spent in Mrs. Gregory's apartment,' answered Maxine Popple, earnestly. 'He usually came when Mr. Gregory was out.'

'I see,' said Hardy. 'Was it Mr. or Mrs. Gregory who arranged the burglary with you?'

Popple, until then in complete repose, let his mouth drop open. His wife drew in a hiss of breath and tightened her lips. Behind her glasses her eyes were like flashes of light. There was something in her expression very different from anything Cellini had seen before, the whole character of her face seemed to change because of the way her cheeks puckered as her lips were drawn in.

On that instant, Cellini knew why the man at the window had seemed so familiar. He was like this woman; younger, smoother, but the forehead and chin were unmistakably the same.

Popple did not even try to speak.

'It is a monstrous accusation,' declared his wife, her voice sharpening to a higher key. 'How dare you—'

'How is your son, Mrs. Popple?' inquired Cellini, pleasantly.

She turned to him, as astounded as her husband had been.

'*Son?*'

'Your son,' said Cellini. 'The man who was at the window of Mrs. Gregory's room the night before last.'

'I—I—I don't know what you mean,' she faltered. 'Why— why should—' She broke off, gulping, while Popple, moving unsteadily, dropped into a chair and buried his face in his hands. Hardy gave a broad, satisfied smile; Cellini had never seen him so pleased.

'All right, Mrs. Popple,' he said. 'You know that I am a police officer. It is my duty to charge that in the early hours of the morning of the day before last you allowed entry to be made into this house for the purpose of allowing certain goods to be stolen. And it is my duty to warn you that anything you say may be written down and produced as

evidence in Court. And Benjamin Popple, it is my duty to
charge that you aided and abetted ... '

*   *   *

In the back parlour were photograph albums, and in
several were photographs of the Popples' son, whose name
was Frederick.

Within half-an-hour of the charge, a general call went out
for the detention of Frederick Popple, who was found in his
home in Lee Road, Hammersmith, not far from the Chiswick
Flyover. He was caught completely unawares. Some of the
smaller *objets d'art* taken from Hethersett were found in
the house, and he made no attempt to deny his part in the
theft and no attempt to withhold information. The leader of
a gang of men who had carried out the raid was a Lancelot
Grey, an antique dealer with many contacts in the United
States and throughout the world, with an address in Putney
Hill. Grey was arrested in his home, and one after another
the members of the gang were rounded up. The largest of
the stolen treasures were in a warehouse in Wandsworth,
none of them damaged. Before midnight, all the men were
under arrest, and every single piece that had been stolen
had been recovered.

The Popples had talked, freely; they had been sure that
the quarrel between the Gregorys would end up with
Gregory storming off and Dr. Selwin giving Melinda a sedative. Indeed, Popple had telephoned his son to give the
all-clear.

But no one had dreamt Selwin would send for Cellini;
and the resultant delay had nearly been disastrous. In fact,
one man had appeared at Melinda's window, expecting to
see no one inside, and intent on climbing in.

And at half-past eleven that night, Cellini called Gregory
at his club.

'I want to talk to you at your home, Mr. Gregory,' he

said. 'It is extremely urgent that you and your wife should answer some questions together.'

Gregory began to protest, but Cellini said firmly, 'It will be in your own interest, I assure you,' and he rang off.

Almost at once Cellini telephoned Melinda, who answered almost before the first ring.

'Who is that?'

'This is Dr. Cellini—'

'I can't stay here alone!' she cried. 'The damned police have arrested the Popples, who wouldn't hurt a fly and there's no one here. You said you had to see me but I tell you—'

'Be quiet!' ordered Cellini, sharply; and as if amazed, she stopped.

'I will be with you in less than an hour,' said Cellini. 'Your husband will be with me. There is an extremely important matter to be discussed. Please wait up.'

'I'll be in my rooms, I won't come downstairs!'

'Lock yourself in if you wish,' urged Cellini, and rang off.

He drove his shiny car much more quickly than usual across London, anxious to be at Hethersett before Gregory, and in fact beat him, though only by five minutes. The lights of Gregory's car swung into the carriageway and shone on Cellini as he began to step down from the car. The big man came swinging across, and they met on the porch.

'What the devil's all this about?' demanded Gregory. 'If this is some damned trick of my wife's—'

'It isn't a trick, and your wife knows no more about it than you do,' said Cellini. 'And if for once you could behave like a civilised human being instead of like a barbarian we might finish our business more quickly, and I could get home reasonably early. Have you a key to the house?'

'Yes,' said Gregory, suddenly meek; and he took out his keys and opened the door.

There were lights on in the hall and on the staircase, as

well as on the landings and passages, making the place look garish; the emptiness of the floors and walls seemed more alarming by night. They reached Melinda's room and Cellini tapped and called out. After a moment the door opened a crack, and she peered through.

'I am here with your husband,' Cellini announced.

She unchained and unbolted the door and opened it wide enough for them to step through. Chairs were round a table, glasses and a variety of drinks were out, a percolator was bubbling, and there were dishes containing biscuits and cheese. The lighting was very bright, and she said frankly, 'I'm afraid of my own shadow. Did *you* know the Popples had been arrested, Bob?'

'The *Popples*? The police must be mad!' Gregory gasped, then glowered at Cellini, 'Unless you had anything to do with it?'

'I had a little,' stated Cellini, not without pride. 'The simple truth is that the Popples were involved in the burglary.' He talked over Gregory's exclamation of astonishment and Melinda's obvious disbelief, and went on, 'A well-known art and antique dealer was the organiser of the raid, and thanks to information supplied by the Popples, all the men involved have been arrested and charged.'

Gregory gasped, 'My *God*! And the stolen treasures?' He could hardly speak for excitement.

'They have all been recovered,' Cellini assured him. 'They will be brought here as soon as the police have carried out some formalities, such as your proof of ownership.' Again he talked over exclamations and expressions of excitement, incredulity, astonishment and delight, but somehow his quiet voice compelled the Gregorys to listen to him. They sat side by side, so obviously overjoyed that it seemed almost a pity to distract them from this delight, but Cellini went on without a change of tone, 'The police will give you all the official information. I am here in the capacity of your psychiatric consultant. Mrs. Gregory, much doubt can be cast on Mrs. Popple's statement about Dr. Selwin's unprofessional conduct with you. Have you any positive recollection? Or did you base your accusation on Mrs. Popple's information?'

Huskily, Melinda said, 'Yes, I did. What a bitch I am.'

'Dr. Selwin's future will be assured provided you make no charge, and spread no rumours,' Cellini said, and after a pause, went on, 'May I assume you will make none?'

'You may,' said Melinda, quite penitently.

'I am sure you will be well-advised.' Cellini sat up very straight. 'Both of you in your different ways have asked me to help you. I do not think your motives have been wholly altruistic and in fact I have been quite repelled by your attitudes, by each of you in turn. I will tell you now that I get little satisfaction out of proving that any human being is insane, and I will also tell you that in my professional opinion each of you is quite *compos mentis*. I trust that is not too great a disappointment to either of you.'

They looked at each other, each touched with embarrassment and perhaps with shame.

'Now I think I should talk to you as to two wholly sane human beings,' went on Cellini. 'I do not know for what reason but your wife, Mr. Gregory, has for many years encouraged you to believe that she had taken lover after lover, whereas in fact these lovers are figments of her imagination. She has at most had an occasional *affaire*.' He paused long enough for Gregory to utter a strangled gasp, before going on, 'It is not good for a woman to have such an unsatisfactory sex life. It causes varying degrees of mental imbalance, evil temper, spitefulness and even malevolence and malice which do great harm both to the woman and to her close relatives and companions. Nor is it good for a man to restrict his sex life. You, Mr. Gregory, have obviously preferred to, rather than to seek constant sexual satisfaction outside your marriage, although few men would have been more justified.'

Husband and wife were staring at each other: as if each was seeing the other for the first time.

'So,' went on Cellini, 'each of you for many years has been as lonely as the damned. I neither know nor care what began this estrangement. I do know that if either of you is to lead a reasonably happy, unfrustrated and fulfilled life from now on, you need to live together as man and wife in all respects.'

He stood up.

He saw their hands clasp.

He turned round; and they did not notice him.

He went out of the room, as they began to reach for each other.

He let himself out and did not look back.

* * *

Two weeks later, Melinda telephoned Cellini. At first, she was diffident, even nervous; she hoped that when Cellini had first gone to see her, she hadn't been too brazen. She had had such moods of wantonness, but none since she and Robert—

'I recall nothing at all that was untoward,' Cellini assured her.

'You are that rare creature,' she said huskily, 'a good man.' Then her voice changed and she became very matter-of-fact. They had all their treasures back, and were having a house-warming in a few days' time. Would he, Dr. Cellini, come with Superintendent Hardy for a kind of preview? They, meaning Bob and herself, wanted Cellini in particular to select any single piece from the collection as a memento of his visits to them. There was, added Melinda, a small goblet wrought by the original Cellini, in gold, and if Dr. Cellini would please accept it ...

When he collected this treasure of all treasures, Cellini was welcomed by Melinda and Bob Gregory together. They looked as if they had never exchanged a cross word in their lives.